HIDDEN SHIFTER

N GRAY

BOOKS

By N Gray

Shifter Days, Vampire Nights & Demons in Between

Twisted

Lady Hawk and Her Mountain Man

Hidden Shifter

Wolf

Wolf Retreat

Night Hunter

The Fixer

Kai

Lee

Flynn

Jude

Scout Thorne

The Secret Tomb

Murder of Crows

Blaire Thorne

Ulysses Exposed

Voodoo Priest

Butterflies and Hurricanes

Salvation

Underworld Legacy

The Dana Mulder Suspense Thriller Series

Deadly Pattern

Devil Mountain

Chasing Evil

Nightcrawler

Horror

What's for Dinner

Creature Features

Monster Features

Thrillers

Lady Killer

More from N Gray

writing as Natalie Michaels

Steve Campbell Psychological Suspense Thrillers

The Last Girl

The Bone Forest

The White Dahlia

I See You

Death in the City

More from N Gray

writing as SD Syns

The Diaries

Red Lace Diaries

www.ngraybooks.com

Vinci Books

vinci-books.com

Published by Vinci Books Ltd in 2026

1

The publisher and the author have made every effort to obtain permissions
for any third party material used in this book and to comply with copyright
law. Any queries in this respect should be brought to the attention of the
publisher and any omissions will be corrected in future editions.
A CIP catalogue record for this book is available from the British Library.
Paperback ISBN: 9781036702199
The EU GPSR authorised representative is Logos Europe, 9 rue Nicolas
Poussion, 17000 La Rochelle, France contact@logoseurope.eu

Chapter One

AVA

I couldn't explain it. This place was where I preferred to come and expel all the bad I'd gone through. I'd hike a trail at least once a week and hoped to catch an animal in its natural habitat. And, if the conditions were right, snap a picture of the beautiful creature. Then I'd watch the sunset; the sky painted in bright colors as the air cooled my warm skin, and the tension I'd clung to all week would dissolve.

Coming here was better than therapy, for me of course. I'd sit on the ground, surrounded by nature and absorbed the sounds, smells and everything my eyes saw.

Some thought I was antisocial, but I was selective of those I brought into my life.

I had to be.

I sucked in a deep breath of air, closed my eyes and allowed the cool breeze to caress my cheeks. My cellphone vibrated, snapping me out of my calm thoughts.

I hated cellphones, but it was a necessity in today's world; and only for emergencies. I had no social media and used my phone only to make work calls.

I glanced at the name displayed on the screen and unfortunately; I had to answer the call. "Hi," I said, trying not to sound irritated.

"Ava, where are you?" Derek asked. He was one of the nicest bosses I'd ever had, but painfully forgetful. I'd tell him I was grabbing lunch, and he'd phone asking for the writeup for the picture I'd sent through. Sometimes I had to leave sticky notes over his desk to remind him which story went with which picture.

"I'm hiking this weekend, remember. I want to take photos for next week's wildlife piece."

"Oh, yeah," Derek said, sounding lost in thought.

I heard him scratch his head. He had a nervous tick where he scratched the back of his head, leaving red welts on his skin, and sometimes his hair fell out. When he did this, he knew he'd forgotten something.

"It's an important piece. You know it's my dream to work for National Geographic. If I get the shots I need, I'm sending them my portfolio." I already had my degree in photography and journalism, and my portfolio was almost complete. I needed this weekend to get some of my best shots to package the portfolio for them. Ever since I was a little girl, I'd wanted to work for National Geographic. All it took was their show on the ocean to get me hooked for life. I wanted to do everything possible to help my chances. They received many applications on a monthly basis, which meant they only selected the best. And I had to be the best.

"Yes, yes, of course. It slipped my mind. I take it you're staying there the weekend?"

"Yes!" I said frustratingly; Derek paid my salary, and I needed to play nice if I wanted to stay in his employ. "You know I can't get the best shot in only a day. I need to stay here, blend in with nature and wait for the animal to come to me."

Silence filled the air, and I rolled my eyes. I shouldn't lose my temper with him. He was actually an amiable person; it was just... sometimes... I needed a break.

"What's wrong?" I asked delicately. It sounded like he was having another bad day and I shouldn't take my frustration out on him—he had enough of his own issues.

"Nothing, there's a dinner with my folks this evening and I was wondering if you wanted to join me. But if you're there, then that's your answer, I guess."

I knew he shrugged to accompany that loud sigh.

"Perhaps next time." I lied. I always said, *'next time'*. Besides, he wasn't my type, he led an unhealthy lifestyle, and he was my boss.

"Okay." Silence filled the space again. "I'll see you Monday then."

"Yes, I'll see you first thing on Monday. Enjoy the dinner and your weekend." I hung up before he said anything else.

I switched off my cellphone and pocketed it. I pressed the fob, my car's alarm sounded and locked.

During the time I was speaking with Derek, three more cars had parked with the occupants going to the various trails they'd be hiking. Two people headed toward the one I was taking.

Once my backpack was on, I headed toward the start of the tough trail; I hadn't hiked it yet, and the ranger assured me the views were breathtaking and the best this time of year. It was also their busiest weekend and she was expecting at least two hundred hikers to come and go. The ranger had pointed out I'd be able to see most of the animals, which were scarce on the other trails.

I'd been coming to Sterling Meadow Forest for a few months and hadn't hiked the harder path because it took much longer and I'd have to spend the entire weekend completing it. The other paths were quick trails and completed in a day.

But I needed the trail where the animals were to get spectacular shots for my portfolio. I kept changing the photos in the portfolio because I didn't think they were good enough and I needed to finish it. My clock wasn't ticking, but I had to stop over analyzing my work, get it done, and send it off. And this weekend I had to get it sorted.

An animal cried, stopping me. I glanced over my shoulder and still saw my vehicle in the parking lot. The cries sounded again, reminding me of a wounded animal. I couldn't continue on my hike until I knew the animal was safe. If it was a predator, I hoped I could run faster.

Pushing through bushes, I came to a clearing where a deer fawn was sitting beside its mother's carcass. My heart broke staring at the poor baby, taking me to the first time I watched Bambi. There was no way I'd allow the fawn to remain on its own and dialed Ruth's number. She was a wildlife veterinarian I'd befriended when I needed to understand animal anatomy.

I didn't approach the fawn for fear of it running off, instead I waited in silence nearby for nearly forty minutes. When a loud noise sent birds flying, I stood slowly from my spot, keeping an eye on the fawn and sauntered to the path. The fawn didn't budge, but she watched me.

Ruth approached with her equipment and two assistants.

"Thanks for coming. I didn't want to leave her on her own," I said, closing the gap. "She looks to be a few days old and I suspect the mom died soon after giving birth." I didn't say I suspected something with large teeth had attacked the mother. When I'd first seen the fawn, I noted the mother had a bite on her neck but couldn't get closer for fear of scaring the baby away. Whichever predator did that had bitten the mother and left, which was incredibly cruel.

"Hi, Ava." Ruth handed her equipment to the girl on her left and hugged me. "You did the right thing calling me. I'll check her out to see if she's healthy, then hand her over to the sanctuary for rehabilitation."

"Thanks."

Ruth had shocking red hair and blue eye shadow. She wore a pink blouse, dark green pants, and green Crocs. Each wrist bound with leather bracelets and a crystal pendant hung around her neck. She was eccentric, easygoing and a loving veterinarian.

"Do you mind if I continue?" I pointed toward the path.

"Oh heavens, yes, of course. When you're done with your hike, you must come visit. I'd love to see your portfolio." She winked.

"Will do." We hugged, and I left them to do what they did best.

The winding path took me around one of the largest mountains in the area and the sights were breathtaking. I stopped near a spring and sat on a fallen log. The spring water was cool and drinkable. I splashed water on the back of my neck and wiped the sweat away with my bandana.

I glanced at my watch and I'd only been walking for two hours. The sun would set soon and I needed to find a place to set up camp before dark. I picked up my backpack and continued on my way.

It didn't take long for the sky to be painted in bright colors. Within twenty minutes the blues and blacks had taken over, bathing the path in dark shadows.

I stopped at an area not used in a while, but it would have to do. The ground was level enough for my tent, with sand and an old log for a fire. Since some animals came out at night, I decided against hiking in the dark, and I didn't want to spook them.

The ranger had mentioned the first main campsite, but it was much farther up the trail. By waiting for Ruth to arrive and tend to the fawn, I started on the path late. But I'd do it again. I couldn't leave the fawn on her own. Anyway, I hardly mingled with other hikers anyway, so the thought of camping out here alone was fine with me.

I removed my backpack and set up camp. The tent was up with a flick of my wrist; I unrolled the sleeping bag and placed it inside. I gathered enough firewood to make a decent fire for warmth and made some tea. For dinner I'd already prepared a chicken wrap at home, followed by a packet of chips.

I connected my cellphone to the portable charger and switched it on. Derek had left messages. He was sweet, but *no*. I vowed never to date my boss… again.

My previous boss/lover owned one of the larger wildlife magazines, and I was his star photographer—or he had made me believe that I was. I travelled the world getting the best pictures, but when his possessive streak worsened, I saw less of him. The result was fewer travels, but frequent visits to the ER. I knew I'd made a mistake getting involved with him; he was not a nice man. Instead of trying to go through the legal battles with the proof I had, it was easier for me to pack my bag. Naturally, he didn't approve and tried to *win* me back by stalking me. I'd gotten away one late evening, and he didn't have a clue where I was.

I found a small town, Krystal Creek, near Sterling Meadow, which I now called home. After a while he'd stopped calling me, and I didn't need to look over my shoulder everywhere I went. But I needed to know where he was and learned he started dating another girl, who was just as crazy as he was if the newspaper articles were to be believed. And exactly a year later I hadn't heard from him.

Once I'd arrived in Krystal Creek, I took a six-month sabbatical, then when I was ready to work again I found a job at the local newspaper/magazine in Krystal Creek. There were two reporters, myself, and Derek, who was the owner and Editor-in-Chief. Derek came from a long line of heirs to the oil industry, but he preferred to spend his inheritance on the Krystal Creek newspaper and seemed to manage the advertising just fine. I got paid per animal photograph, special features, or anything worthy of the space.

I read the text messages Derek had sent, and they were the usual ones; *'Let me know if you change your mind'*, *'I'll send my driver to fetch you'* and *'Wish you were here'*. He really wanted me with him, but I couldn't. I didn't have the heart to say *'No'*, but I wondered whether it was for the best. Then again, I might lose the only income I had if I told Derek I wasn't interested.

I sighed and deleted his texts. It was better to avoid. I would deal with it on Monday. Right now, I wanted to enjoy nature in all her splendor with only myself to keep me company, which I preferred. It wasn't as if I didn't want anyone in my life, I did, but the next guy would have to be worth it.

Chapter Two

AVA

Splashing from waterfalls and swimming woke me, but it was only my aching bladder. I unzipped my tent, crawled out and grabbed tissues and a disposable bag.

I didn't want to go near my tent or the path. I ventured a short distance farther into the dense vegetation with the silver moon as my guide. Once I found a spot void of thorns and bushes, I squatted and relieved my bladder.

When done, I covered the wet spot with sand and packed the used tissue in the disposable bag I'd throw away when I reached a trashcan at the main campsite.

Glistening water caught my attention, and I turned in the direction of the rushing river. I'd never seen it so clear before. The other hiking trails seemed to miss the views of the river completely, and with the moon reflecting on the water, it was a sight to behold.

When I turned to retrace my steps, I couldn't figure out which way to go. I traversed through brushes on my left and when I didn't reach my tent; I backtracked. I ended up at the same spot I'd seen the river and walked straight up the mountain. Again, my tent was nowhere in sight. I turned around to get to the area near the river, but when I didn't find it, panic settled in. I closed my eyes and pinched my nose. I tried to steady my breathing and when that didn't work; I carried on walking. I'd never gotten so disorientated before that I'd lost my campsite. Next time I'd pack string to find my way back.

When bright light caught my attention, I exhaled thinking it was the fire at my campsite but then I remembered I'd killed the fire before I went to sleep. Someone else was here.

I carefully rounded a thorn bush, but my shirt hooked on it. I tugged, got free, but ripped the material.

Sounds caught my attention, and I neared.

Peering around a tree I saw a fire blazing, the red, orange and yellow flames hypnotizing. But that's not what caught my attention. I watched him lean on his elbows, kissed the woman's neck and thrusted inside her. His ass cheeks clenched as he moved above her. He kissed her gently yet passionately down the slopes of her breasts. She moaned and writhed beneath him.

Oh, my gods.

I felt my cheeks heat and crossed my legs. My jaw slackened as I stared at their sensual lovemaking.

It was not right to watch. I should feel guilty and a little dirty, but I didn't. There was something beautiful watching this couple—it was raw and sensual. She lay on a blanket, her long dark hair pooled beneath her, her arms clutching onto him as he drove himself into her; over and over. The man was tanned and much bigger than his partner. He had short, neat hair, with muscles in all the right places; they moved with such dexterity—like liquid metal.

My core tightened as I watched him. His rhythm quickened, she whimpered in pleasure and I watched with bated breath.

I couldn't look away; I didn't have the willpower to leave. I only regretted not having my camera with me—they were irresistible, their heavenly bodies entwined as they made love.

I bit my lip as my inner muscles clenched, seeking my release.

My hand slipped down the front of my shirt and into my shorts. I was so turned on it wouldn't take me long. It had been months since I'd had stimulation by my hand, and a year by another. It was by choice. If I ever dated again, it would be different. It had to be.

I leaned my shoulder against the tree to free my other hand and pinched an aching nipple.

I bit my lip again as the man grunted his satisfaction while she writhed and moaned, but he didn't stop—he brought her to the edge then slowed as he eased himself out of her then slipped back inside. He sucked on her nipple and I pinched mine. I wanted to feel his hot breath against my chilled skin, his teeth grazing my nipple, and I pinched the other one. I wanted his weight to crush my body, limiting my movement as he drove deeper.

The man quickened his thrusts, and I pushed a finger inside my wet slit as I imagined his large member pushed deep inside me.

Their grunting and moans were music to my ears as I neared the edge of my release.

When silence filled the air, my eyes focused on his deep blue gaze.

My veins filled with ice. My heart thundered in my chest.

He continued staring.

He'd seen me. He knew I'd been watching. He caught me with my hands in my pants.

Oh my gods. What have I done?

He sniffed the air and grinned. His dark gaze penetrated mine and I felt as naked as the woman beneath him.

"What's wrong?" asked the woman as she peered over his shoulder.

I had to get away. I had to find my tent, pack and leave.

I dashed from the tree before the woman saw me.

The forest was dark; the silver moon hid behind black clouds. A thorn bush pricked my face, causing me to cry out. I staggered away from the thorn bush and into a copse —one I'd never noticed before. Somehow I'd gotten turned around and was moving in a new direction. The faster I ran, the farther I went away from my camp, I was sure of it.

Leaves crushed behind me.

He was chasing me, and he was catching up.

The sounds of grunts and a low growl as he neared.

An animal?

I glanced over my shoulder at two glowing yellow eyes. I yelped and ran faster.

My ankle twisted and I collided with something hard. I saw darkness, something snapped behind me, and a weight-lessness seeped into my bones.

Chapter Three

TYLER

After last night's excitement and finding that girl in our forest, our clan was on high alert. Then Blaze cornered me to let me know he'd found *something*. The last thing we needed was something else to set everyone on edge. Fortunately, he'd come to me first and not our chieftain or all hell would break loose and they'd blame the poor girl.

I followed Blaze to the spot where he'd seen the carcasses of five deers. Their remains were scattered as if trying to flee the chaos. Each animal had their guts ripped out by sharp claws; the ground beneath their bodies a mess of organs and blood. One deer had their eyes gorged out.

"Jesus," I breathed as I crouched near the carcass. "We needed these animals for our full moon feast."

"Whoever is doing this is messing with our food." Blaze combed his fingers through shaved hair, I think he did it out of frustration or habit. He'd shaved his head when he struggled to get the knots out of his long hair. "Do you think one of us did it or there's another were-animal hunting this side?"

"I don't know, but we need to find out before Ash hears."

Blaze growled.

"Don't worry, we'll find out who did it. In the meantime, clean this up?"

"Sure."

I left Blaze to sort that out and pushed down the images of the grotesque scene. It sent my imagination running.

I headed toward the huts when Windtalker waved me down. He was our healer within the clan and spiritual advisor.

"Tyler, what have you been up to?" he asked. His one eye narrowed down on me while the other remained large and unmoving. He'd had an accident when he was young and hadn't seen out of it since. His tanned skin leathery, and his silver hair cascaded around his shoulders.

"I thought you already knew?" I arched an eyebrow. He usually came to us before we did something foolish, pointing a crooked finger in our face, and warning us not to do it.

"Something happened last night," he said hoarsely, like he'd been screaming at dancers all night.

"Did you finally get laid?"

Windtalker slapped my shoulder and shook his head. "Silly boy, not me… You." He slid his crooked fingers around my bicep and squeezed. "Come see me when you *feel it*," he said cryptically, let go of my arm and hobbled away on his walking stick.

Unsure which plant Windtalker had smoked, I would ignore the strange conversation for now, and headed toward the hut where last night's voyeur was sleeping. As much as I loved someone, especially a beautiful someone, watching me have sex, I needed to understand what she was doing here. If this woman was part of a group of hunters in our part of the forest, I needed to find out, and if not, what was she doing off the hiking trail?

Chapter Four

AVA

Everything ached. I couldn't be certain of the location of the pain; whether it was my ankle, my hip, or my head—or it was my entire body.

The last thing I remembered was running in the dark.

I jackknifed out of bed, but when a surge of pain shot through my hip and neck, I stopped moving. My vision blurred and pressure built up in my head, forcing me to lie back down. I kept my eyes open as my head spun and slowly the ceiling came into focus.

I stared up at a wooden roof, with a wooden wall to my right. The bed beneath me felt soft and furry.

"How are you feeling?" said someone with a deep baritone.

My arms pebbled at the sound of his voice. I coughed to clear my throat, swallowed hard, and slowly turned my head. I narrowed my eyes at him.

My heart stopped when I saw him; his honed body, his hair cut short and those same piercing blue eyes. His face was pleasant with a sharp nose, kissable lips and defined jaw. My heart skipped a beat as his dark gaze raked over my body, and my cheeks heated. Flashes of his naked ass as he pumped into that woman heated me from my core. His eyes held a hint of humor, as if knowing I'd just thought about him.

Oh, crap.

He knew I'd watched him having sex, and he saw me touching myself. I'd die from embarrassment if I wasn't already in so much pain.

"What are you doing here?" he grumbled in that deep baritone that could set women's panties on fire. He sounded exotic and scary at the same time; a lethal combination for any woman.

"I take pictures… I got lost… and I stumbled upon…" I swallowed hard and blinked slowly. I sounded like a blubbering idiot. I swallowed and tried again. "I'm a photographer and was camping in the area. I lost my way after using the… you know… bathroom," I said, keeping my eyes closed for fear of losing track of my thoughts.

He grunted. I didn't think he believed me.

Wood creaked. I opened my eyes and glanced in his direction again, and he sat back in the chair. He was naked from the waist up and wore tattered jeans, and no shoes. His body thrummed with power I couldn't imagine, leaving me wondering if he was a shifter or something else. My insides twisted; I was strangely afraid and aroused at once.

I caught glints of silver in his dark hair, which meant nothing. An old school friend had been gray since she was in her early twenties.

"We couldn't locate your camp." His statement a silent question. I didn't understand what he was alluding to, but I would try to talk my way out of it. I meant no one harm.

I pushed up on my elbows and slowly sat up, leaning my back and head against the wooden wall. My vision tunneled, and when I focused again I paid attention to my surroundings. The small room had a bed, a fireplace in one corner, and a small shower/toilet area. Everything was made from wood, including the bed frame. The bedding was animal fur. It was primitive and beautiful.

I focused my attention on the man again. "I don't even know where we are. There's no way I can tell you where my tent is. I camped near the path—"

"The hiking trail?"

I nodded.

"You're way off course."

"You'd think."

A growl escaped his lips.

I shot a frightened glance his way, blinked, and then he stood beside me. I hadn't heard or seen him move from the creaking chair, yet he now stood awfully close to me; so close I could smell him; musk, soap, and a hint of sweat.

He pointed a finger, inches from my face. "We don't like wanderers. And I don't trust you." He stood taller and his chest heaved; as if controlling his anger. "If it wasn't for your injuries, I would've walked you to the trail myself. But—"

"I'm fine. I'll just be on my way." I didn't want to stay here, anyway. I'd much rather leave. I swung my legs off the bed, and tried to stand. Pain seared through my body causing me to sway.

"Clearly you're not fine." He clenched his jaw.

"I'm okay. Do you have a stick I could lean on?" I wanted to get back to my campsite, pack and leave. "I have pain medication in my backpack."

I felt powerful hands on my shoulders as he pushed me

back onto the bed, lifting my legs and gently set them on the bed.

"You can leave when you can stand without swaying. Get some rest. I'll send someone to give you food."

His mood confused me, one moment he sounded ready to rip my head off, the next he sounded caring.

"What's your name?" I asked, but he had already left.

I didn't know where I was or who they were. I didn't know anyone even lived in this forest. I'd known about the various shifter territories where the forest split equally for each shifter animal. But this part of the forest was for hikers only. No were-animal lived here. Or so I'd thought.

At least they didn't hurt me or leave me in the forest to suffer from my injuries. Knowing my luck, I'd probably stay lost.

I eased myself to a seated position to assess what hurt. I stared at my legs; they'd bandaged my right ankle with a type of brown banana leaf. I'd either twisted or broken my ankle; it was swollen and blossomed a lovely shade of purple. I still wore the T-shirt I'd torn and shorts but they were dirty, and on my right hip mud caked. I wiped away the dirt and winced, I must've fallen on something hard when I'd hit my head running into something. I felt the large egg-shaped bruise on the right side of my forehead, wincing. Served me right for watching them have sex.

Slowly I swung my legs off the bed and stood, but my weight was too much for my ankle. I wanted to see what I looked like, but the tiny mirror was on the other side of the room. I had nothing to help me cross the room with. I'd look when I could walk there. For now, I'd have to live with my current state. Nobody cared what I looked like out here, anyway.

I sighed and climbed back onto the bed. I needed at least another day to recover; the bruising to come down and able to stand without the dizziness. It was possible I had a concussion, but unless I saw a doctor, I wouldn't know.

Chapter Five

TYLER

I pointed at Miles, who ran to assist me.

"I need you to give her food. Some pieces of meat, bread, and water should be fine."

"Okay, sure. Anything else?"

"Make sure she doesn't leave. I don't want her wandering around."

"Yes, Tyler." Miles darted in the opposite direction toward the kitchen area.

Ash stood outside his hut with his arms folded, wearing a grim expression. Claw sat near his feet like the sniveling bastard he was. I knew what Ash was going to say. I raised my hand as I approached, and he closed his mouth.

"I know, Father. I shouldn't have brought her here."

"Then why did you?"

I didn't know why I brought her here. She had injured herself. If I had left her where she'd fallen, she would either succumb to her wounds or the wild animals would've gotten to her. I didn't have to bring her here... yet I did.

I glanced over my shoulder at the hut she was in and my

saber fought for release. He'd smelled her arousal last night, and he loved her sweet scent. He almost ripped Cheryl to shreds when he smelled the other female. I didn't even get to finish, and it left me frustrated. But my saber wanted to chase the other woman; he ached to run free now. *Easy cat.* My beast shuddered beneath my skin. I pushed him down, ensuring I kept in control.

"She injured herself and I couldn't leave her out there. What if the bears got to her?"

"So, what? We don't care about humans, Tyler, and you know this," Ash grumbled.

It was the same conversation Father and I always had. He hated humans, while I encouraged interaction. If we wanted to increase our numbers, we had to look for mates outside the clan. We only had three single females and six single males, and none of the females wanted any of the men as partners. No mate meant no kittens. And to make matters worse, the couples weren't producing offspring either, and nobody knew why. There was one other saber pack, but they were too far and didn't want to join us. Our only viable alternative included human women, but my father didn't approve. He wanted nothing to do with them. Hence we had a problem nobody could fix, and until then, our pack stayed small.

"Her being here is going to cause trouble within our pack," Ash stated, bringing me out of my thoughts.

If I smelled her scent, so would the other males. She was human, beautiful, and ripe for the picking. The moon would soon be at its fullest which made our beasts savage animals and having a woman, like her around, resulted in fighting between us. But it spelled trouble for her; she'd have males crashing through the door trying to claim her. The next two days were going to be a nightmare, but Miles and Blaze would help me.

"What are you going to do, Tyler?" He continued like a broken record. As our fearless leader, he hardly had answers.

"This weekend is their busiest, and there's no way I can take her to her car without being seen. Give her a couple of days to heal, then I'll escort her to the trail myself. And I'll keep the others away."

"Until then, she stays inside. Miles keeps watch and I don't want her walking around. And I don't want her seeing our people."

I nodded my understanding.

"In the meantime, find her camp and bring her things here. She couldn't have been too far when she stumbled upon you." Ash's lips quirked in amusement. He'd laughed so hard when I'd told him how she saw me. Cheryl wasn't pleased when I returned with another woman in my arms. She hadn't spoken to me since last night.

"And take Claw with you."

I narrowed my eyes at the bastard on the ground and grunted. The best thing for me to do was to ignore him.

"The last thing we need is a rescue party searching the forest for her," I said, ignoring Ash's request.

"Exactly." Ash turned on his heel and entered his hut.

Chapter Six

TYLER

I approached the hut where Miles stood like a security guard; he scowled at nothing with crossed arms over his broad chest.

"Don't look so serious." It was hard seeing him as a serious person without a shirt on, torn shorts, and barefoot.

He shook out his arms and shrugged. "Only doing my job," he said with a lopsided grin.

"Did she eat?"

"She's busy now."

I slapped his shoulder and knocked on the door. I didn't want to intrude if she was in the bathroom.

"Yeah?" she said meekly.

I opened the door slowly. She sat on the bed with her back against the wall; her injured leg straight on the bed while the other tucked beneath her. She had the plate propped on her lap and I'd caught her mid-bite.

I stared at her; long, curly hair the color of chestnuts, youthful porcelain skin and chocolate-colored eyes that glistened in the dim light. She was absolutely breathtaking.

My beast pushed to the front for a taste, and I shoved him back down. *Not yet, you animal.*

She eyed me suspiciously as she slowly nibbled on the bread. She squeezed her hand around the knife handle, I should've told Miles not to give her any cutlery.

"I want to find your campsite and bring your things here. Can you think of any markers?"

She unclenched the knife in her hand, her shoulders dropped slightly and she exhaled.

Did she think I was going to hurt her? I ignored the thought.

She was quiet for a moment, chewed, then finally answered. "I'd hiked about six miles yesterday and came to an area where the ground was flat enough for my tent. I don't remember any other markers. It's before the main camp area. Sorry, it's the first time I'd hiked the route and don't remember anything else."

I knew the area she referred to and nodded. "I know the place. You wandered off quite a distance. We're about two miles from there."

"Two miles? Jeez, I don't know how I got so lost. All I did was use the bathroom and then somehow... But how on earth could I have walked two miles. It felt like a short distance."

I chuckled, remembering the look on her face when I'd caught her gawking at me with her hand in her pants and the other under her shirt. I thought of her sweet arousal as it flooded my senses last night, and I felt my cock grow thinking about her touching herself.

"You stumbled upon me only a mile away," I grinned.

Her brows furrowed, then her cheeks blossomed a healthy shade of pink when she remembered how we'd first met.

"Oh my gods." She buried her face in her hands. "I'm

sorry about that, I didn't mean to stare. I hope your girl-friend isn't angry?" she asked sheepishly.

"No-one is angry, and she's not my girlfriend."

"Oh," she glanced at her hands as she fidgeted with the knife. "My name is Ava." She proffered her hand. "I would stand but," — she shrugged, — "you know."

The moment I touched her hand, my body warmed. "Tyler."

Chapter Seven

TYLER

I'd told Claw we'd meet him at his hut so he could come with us, but we didn't. I didn't want the bastard near my father or me, and I certainly didn't want to include him in anything I did. Claw was not my brother, no matter how many times Ash said so.

I left Miles to watch over Ava while Blaze and I headed toward her campsite. It would only take us about thirty minutes to get there, so we didn't think it necessary to shift into our saber beasts. We headed in the direction of the hiking trail we usually avoided.

They had sectioned most of the forest in Sterling Meadow for each of the various were-animals to hunt in. No shifter wanted to get into another's territory and create an unnecessary war.

When they had driven us from our home, we quietly moved here. We'd heard Sterling Meadow had one of the best Master Vampires and they had formed the Were-Animal Alliance, WAA, that included all the different were-animals.

We knew our kind would be safer here, but remained on high alert. Most had thought our were-animal had gone extinct due to the humans hunting and killing us for our fur and large elongated canines. Although hunting was now outlawed, we didn't want to chance it.

There were only two clans left; one was west, the other east. The human population had grown and in need of space, and had driven us apart and out of our land.

We didn't know what would happen if we approached the WAA, or Léon—the Master Vampire. We'd been living undetected on their mountains for two years until last night. We wanted to remain hidden for the safety of our clan, even though we desperately needed females.

"Cheryl's still pissed at you." Blaze pushed branches out of his face, the moment he let go they would've smacked me in the face if I hadn't caught them.

"She'll get over it," I grumbled.

"You need to choose, Tyler. You've gone back to her too many times. You know she wants you."

"I need to find someone I can see myself settling down with, unfortunately she's not that person. You know how it goes."

He nodded. "You're playing with fire, and Cheryl will scratch your eyes out."

"She can try," I chuckled nervously. He was probably right, but I couldn't see myself bonding with her. She was uptight and complained too much. And my father was our clan's chieftain and I his only son. He'd taken over from his father and they expected I would be next in line. And Cheryl hoped to be my partner. But there was no spark between us. I loved her body, and her mind, but there was no earth shattering moments between us. I needed a little more before I settled with only one person. And, for the most important part, my saber didn't want her either.

"You know Ash can't hand his crown over to you unless you've found your mate."

"He will never give up his power."

Ash had become addicted to his seat at the top, and even if I found someone, he wouldn't approve of her just so he didn't have to relinquish his power.

"You know you need to fight him." Blaze eyed me, his way of hinting what I already knew. His sparkling blue eyes sent at least one female swooning, but they did nothing to me.

"You know I can't."

"Because you'll kill him."

I swallowed my answer and continued up the mountain. Ash was a pain in everyone's side, but he was my only family. There's no way I could fight him—and yes, I would kill him.

"Well, here's the path." Blaze broke the awkward silence as we stepped onto the hiking trail.

"She said we'll be able to see her tent from the path."

We still had a short distance before we reached the area I thought she had set up camp. The path was void of hikers, and I silently thanked the gods.

In the distance I saw part of an orange tent behind leafy bushes. I pointed. Blaze stepped off the path, and I followed. Her campsite was where she'd said. Blaze dismantled her tent while I packed her belongings in her backpack.

"She really got lost, didn't she? The moon was bright enough last night for her to see, but she was way off course." Blaze lightheartedly chuckled.

"I don't know what she was doing," I grinned.

"It's as if she's meant to find you," Blaze said and winked when I glanced at him.

"I'm all for a voyeur. The kinkier the better, but I doubt she meant to find me. It was just an accident." I picked up a pen and book, leafed through the pages and realized it was her diary. I slammed it shut and quickly stuffed it into her backpack. The last thing I wanted was her screaming because I'd invaded her privacy. The irony was not lost on me as I smiled at the backpack in my hand.

"Here's her phone," Blazed said, reading whatever was on the screen. "Christ, someone has been trying to get hold of her." Blaze removed the portable charger and handed both items to me.

"She doesn't have a screen lock on her phone?"

"Nope."

Either she didn't care who read her messages or she didn't care for the phone. It wasn't an expensive phone, but still. Most people locked their phones.

I read all twenty-five text messages; a guy named Derek seemed to pester her. I rolled my eyes. The dude was desperate. "Either Derek is an old flame who can't get the hint, or they're together and he wants to see her this weekend."

"Wouldn't he be with her if they were an item?"

"Dunno, maybe? Humans are strange creatures with shortcomings, but we're going to need them if we're to survive. It's just a matter of when and not if." I placed the items in her backpack, zipped it closed, and slung it over my shoulder. "Let's get out of here." I glanced at the site one last time, but we'd picked everything up. "Let's head down there. She said she went this way when she needed to... you know. I want to ensure she dropped nothing someone could find."

We traversed through rough terrain and doubted she'd come this way down. She would've stumbled and knocked herself out long before she'd found her way to me. We headed down a slope, passed an area where one could see the river, and headed home. I couldn't see any disturbance apart from our footsteps.

I didn't know how Ava wound up so lost and so far from her camp. At least we had her stuff and nobody would be looking for her.

We hoped.

Chapter Eight

AVA

The air inside the hut was stifling, and I fanned my face. The dark wooden walls seemed to breathe as they closed in on me. I wiped sweat from my brow and tried to focus on my breathing.

One… two… breathe… three… four… breathe…

There was no way I could stay cooped up inside this tiny hut while I recovered. I craved the freedom to sit and rest somewhere else and at least have a view of the outside world. Staring at these four walls, and the tiny bathroom, was not entertaining but bland and depressing. The bed had become uncomfortable and my body ached. And I couldn't sleep.

The walls crept closer as the dark shadows moved, suffocating me.

Five… six… breathe…

I needed out. Now.

Slowly, I dropped to my knees on the ground and winced. I rested my injured foot on my left ankle and crawled on the floor. They made the hut of wood and on short stilts. I wondered if they did that for the rainy season; the last thing I wanted was mud through my hut. I took another slow creep toward the door and my hip ached from leaning on my right knee. Every part of my right-hand side hurt, and I wondered what I'd hit when I fell. *A rock?*

The swollen egg on my forehead throbbed as I stared down at the floor, taking one slow crawl at a time. My right shoulder felt like it was being pulled out of the socket and my elbow strained to keep my upper body from crashing to the ground.

I felt silly but the dark colors in the hut were depressing; I needed to see some greens and blues. Maybe some orange.

Finally, when I reached the door, I pulled myself up and opened it. The man who'd given me breakfast stood like a security guard. He twisted his body and stared down at me. His blond hair hung in his youthful face, his narrowed green eyes the color of fresh grass with flecks of bright yellow; reminding me of a cat I once owned as a kid. His eyes were a beautiful color and strangely mesmerizing. It took willpower not to gawk at the guy, his honed body hard and beautiful. But I felt nothing for him. I tried to peek around his broad shoulders at the rest of the area, but he blocked my view.

"What are you doing?" he asked, his deep baritone made me swallow my words.

I sucked in a breath of the fresh air and smiled, hopefully I'd put him at ease and myself. "I need fresh air. Please, I'm begging you. Can I sit over there?" I pointed at the chair against the side of the hut. "There's even a chair for me to use."

The man glanced around nervously. When he turned to face me his dark demeanor left my blood chilled.

"No. If my chieftain finds out you are outside the hut

and looking around, he will ask me to bury your corpse. Do you want to die today?"

I shook my head. "No, I'm sorry I'm a pest, but that room," — I thumbed behind me, — "is depressing. I need to see something else; some trees and flowers. I'll even be happy looking at grass. Do you think if you asked permission from your chieftain I could sit somewhere I won't see anyone? You can even blindfold me and lead me out to an area I can sit by myself. I promise I don't mean anyone any harm." My voice broke at the last few words, surprising myself. I wasn't usually emotional and rarely cried, but somehow I felt a little teary today. I blamed the injury and that I couldn't do what I wanted to do. I felt frustrated and caged.

My eyes stung from the moisture, but I didn't want to bring that fact to his attention. Hopefully, he would just ignore it.

He exhaled audibly and shook his head. "Go inside and I'll find out, but I can't leave you unattended. I need to wait for Tyler."

"Thank you. I appreciate it. I really do. And, sorry again." I turned back onto my hands and knees and crawled back to the bed.

"Let me help you."

I yelped when powerful hands picked me up off the floor and carried me like a sleeping child to the bed. He did it with ease, which was a relief. No woman wanted a man picking her up, carrying her like a child, grunting as he complained about her weight.

I giggled as he set me gently onto the bed. "Thanks. What's your name?"

"Miles."

33

"I'm Ava, and nice to meet you, and sorry again." I groaned inwardly, I had to stop apologizing.

"Stay here."

"I will, but please don't forget to ask. My body hurts from lying all the time. I'm very active and sitting still kills me."

"I'll see what I can do."

"That's all I ask. Thank you."

After my ex had used me as a punching bag, I vowed not to let that happen again. I attended self-defense classes, built enough muscle to defend myself, and kept active and healthy. I attended gym classes every day and on my off days I snapped shots of animals. I preferred the company of wild creatures to humans. Some people were cruel while some animals loved you, regardless. When approaching an animal, one had to first assess the situation before closing the distance. An animal was still wild and might hurt you. If you thought you were in danger, it was best to leave the beast alone. One couldn't do that with humans. If you sensed danger and tried to get away, the human would still pounce and hurt you.

I sighed. I still couldn't believe I was in this mess. That's what I got for taking a stroll in the middle of the night, getting lost, and spying on a couple having sex.

Chapter Nine

TYLER

We'd just reached the edge of the village when Miles ran up to us. Something in his face made me uneasy.

"Tyler!" he yelled as he jogged. "She wants to sit outside—"

"What? I hope you told her no."

"Yes, but she's begging for permission. We can blindfold her and take her to a spot away from the village."

My brows furrowed. It was a strange request. "Did you ask Ash?"

Miles closed his mouth and averted his eyes.

Chicken.

"Fine, let me speak with her first before I go to him."

"Thank you."

I stormed into the hut. She shrieked. I dropped her backpack on the bed. She stared with wide eyes but without fear. Her gaze penetrating me—inside my soul. An uneasiness spread throughout as my beast rippled, trying to get out.

"Why do you want to sit outside?" The words sounded

harsh, I only did it for my beast. He wasn't listening to me and needed to understand who was in control. *Easy kitty, we didn't know her.*

"I don't want anyone getting into trouble. It's just I can't stay in here all day long. My body aches from lying and I need to be outside." She pleaded with misty eyes. "You can blindfold me and lead me somewhere away from your people. I have no clue where I am." She sounded defeated. "I don't know who you are or why you're here, nor am I interested in knowing. I'll never tell anyone. Please." Her honey-colored eyes silently begging. It was hard to resist her as I pictured her blindfolded, naked, and on me.

I snapped out of it, pushing my beast where he belonged.

"I can't promise anything."

I left before she answered while Miles stood guard. I didn't want to speak with Ash, but I felt for her. I understood. I needed to be in nature and hated the claustrophobia of walls and the concrete jungle. I needed to surround myself with the outside world. As much as I didn't want to, I related to her need.

I found Ash cleaning fish he'd caught in the river.

Who said cats didn't like water? Technically, we weren't cats in today's sense, like leopards or lions, even though we were much bigger than them. We're closely related to different families of cat-like carnivores, comprising hyenas and mongoose. It's strange but true. Our bulkier sizes shadowed were-leopards and were-lions; even in our human form, we were bigger than our human counterparts.

"What now?" he asked without looking up at me.

He had such a way with words, it still amazed me he was our chieftain.

I cleared my throat. "If I blindfold and carry her a distance away from the clan, would you approve?"

Ash turned and stared at me through irritated and bushy eyebrows. He knew nobody appreciated *this* look, and I fought the urge to laugh. "What are you talking about?"

"She wants to sit outside for a bit. She prefers the company of nature to four wooden walls." I raised my hand to stop him from interrupting me. "I will watch her myself."

"You're too soft, Tyler. I don't know how you're ever going to take over and lead my people," he grunted, turned around and continued scaling the fish. "If I wasn't your chieftain, they would slaughter everybody because you're too *kind*. Perhaps someone else needs to take over when I'm gone."

A growl tore from my lips, and my teeth elongated. My saber was as sick as I was of his taunting. He ignored us and continued cleaning his fish.

"Sometimes kindness is a sign of strength."

Father made a strange strangling noise from the base of his throat. "It's your hide if she escapes and blubbers her big mouth to the others about our existence and whereabouts. Then everybody will know how weak you truly are."

I didn't bother answering him; he knew I was right but would never admit it. He, much like me, loved nature and would stop no one from going outside. Yes, she was human, and yes we risked her dashing off to tell the others about us, but she didn't know our species nor did she know exactly where we were.

"Why didn't you take Claw with you earlier?" he asked as I started walking away.

I'd forgotten about him. I should've known he'd complain to my dad.

"I looked for him, but he must've been hiding away, again."

"Next time, look harder. The poor boy was in tears because you didn't fetch him."

I didn't respond. It was a moot point—and no matter what I said, I'd lose.

Chapter Ten

TYLER

I approached Ava's hut, but Blaze intercepted me. He wore an expression I'd seen before and without words I knew what had happened.

He pointed, I nodded, and we walked in silence.

Once we were outside the perimeter, Blaze spoke. "It happened again." He pointed to a bush. "While you were speaking with Ash, I came across this."

We rounded the bush to a grisly site; two severed deer heads, their guts gouged out, and their eyes and tongues missing.

"What's this white stuff?" I pointed at the hole in one eye socket. It looked like... "Christ, is that what I think it is?"

"Someone masturbated in it. Yeah, I thought the same."

I glanced at the huts and my shoulders tensed. I jerked my chin in that one particular hut's direction, and Blaze followed my line of sight.

"Do you really think it's him?"

"Unfortunately, we didn't take him with us——"

"To fetch the girl's stuff?"

"Yeah."

"So it's true?"

I gave Blaze a curt nod.

"We need to monitor him and Darla, I want to know where they are at all times. And Ash cannot know."

It would be my fault if Ava got hurt. I'd brought her here instead of taking her back to her camp. I could've walked with her in my arms looking for her tent, yet I didn't, I brought her *here*. Somehow I wanted her with me, my beast wanted her, without understanding why. The moment I saw her standing beside the tree I knew I wanted her. *We wanted her.* When I caught her scent, it was a shot of adrenaline, something I hadn't felt before.

And I would protect her.

If Claw approached Ava, I'd kill him.

Chapter Eleven

AVA

The door flew open, hitting the wall. I flinched, almost falling off the bed. I'd been going through the shots I'd taken on my hike yesterday and noted I'd taken a few great shots of trees and birds. I managed not to drop my camera and winced from the sudden movement; wanting to scream, instead I stared daggers at Tyler. His hair hung in his eyes. His naked chest rose and fell as if he was running or trying to control his anger. Either way, I was nervous seeing him like that. I didn't know him or his moods, and perhaps he'd decided he'd had enough of me and was here to kill me.

Yet, something within me wasn't afraid of him. I trusted him to care for me. I was most likely concussed and feeling emotions that weren't real. I'd only just met him, there was no chance I had any feelings for him.

But, every time I saw him, I pictured his naked body and wondered what he felt like as he pumped into me. To have his powerful hands roam over my body. The mere thought of him made me burn with desire.

These thoughts were wrong, obviously, but I couldn't

help it. His magnetism pulled me toward him like no other. It wasn't only his physique and demanding tone, but how I felt when he was near. Or perhaps how my body reacted, like I was about to burst into desirable flames.

I had to get these thoughts out of my head. He was not the person for me.

He had said the woman from last night was not his girl-friend, that told me he played around and unfortunately I was not a toy. If he only liked me that way, I would not give in to him.

I stared at his muscular body, then my eyes flitted to his face; to his piercing blue eyes that held concern. I realized he'd done nothing but care for me. And it wasn't as if I could blurt out my thoughts, he'd think I'd lost my marbles. That didn't mean I couldn't fantasize about the forbidden fruit.

His steady gaze raked up my body from my legs then back to my eyes, unsettling me.

Again sensing a shift in his demeanor, I shuffled to the top of the bed and waited.

We stared at each other.

The silence thundered in my ears.

He didn't move.

I flinched when Tyler raised his fist with something dangling from it. *Material?*

"Can you stand here," — he pointed to where he stood, — "or do you need help?" His deep voice warmed my body and shot straight to my core. I shifted uncomfortably.

"I can try." I climbed off the bed and carefully tested my ankle. Pain shot up my shin and I quickly lifted it.

His hands abruptly gripped my upper body and carried me to the middle of the room. Tyler let go. I tried to stand still but swayed slightly. It was then I realized I was inches away from his chest. I felt heat radiate from him and it was oddly comforting.

His dark gaze a heavy blanket against my chest. I glanced up to meet his deep-blue eyes. They were so pretty, yet I couldn't help but think he was warning me—to stay away from him.

He cleared his throat, and I averted my gaze... to his chest—which was also wrong. I stood so close I smelled *him*; he had an earthy undertone, a hint of sweat and something else I couldn't distinguish. He smelled so good I wanted to lean forward and press my cheek against his hot skin.

Snap out of it! I blinked and pushed the desire away.

His naked body flashed before me and my neck heated, followed by my face—not just my cheeks, my entire face was fiery. I saw his body rock into that woman and I craved it was me beneath him; feeling his strength and impaled by him, repeatedly. I wanted to touch every inch of his body, and him to touch me.

Stop it.

I had to control myself.

I needed to remember I didn't know this man. He most likely had a new woman every night at his disposal. I needed to remind myself I would not be that person. I wanted something meaningful. Something permanent. Something that was right for my soul.

If I had to compare myself to the beauty from last night, I was the complete opposite. My hair was dark and naturally curly, my skin pale and my eyes dark. She was tanned, toned, and sexy. I wore cotton underwear, and I doubted she wore any.

"Can you stand still?" he asked with amusement.

"Uh-huh." My eyes raked up his body and met his eyes again, I smiled.

He moved to stand behind me; I felt the loss of heat from my front and felt it beat against my back. I wondered if I could lean back into his front and stick my ass out.

What is wrong with you? I bit my lip to stop the wanton thoughts.

There was something wrong with me. I'd never had these thoughts about anyone before, let alone a man I'd just met and lived in the forest. It was strange they did that, and I surmised they were shifters, hiding from everyone.

Without warning, the soft material touched my face as he tied it over my eyes, rendering me sightless.

The action was erotic and left me a quivering puddle. My heart thundered in my chest. I couldn't see but felt his heat envelope me. It was uncomfortable, yet strangely alluring. With my senses muddled, I tried to stand on my injured ankle without falling over. But what threw me was the need to touch him, to feel him beneath me.

Gods, something's wrong with me. I had hit my head extremely hard to think of him this way.

"I can smell your desire, Ava," he breathed near the shell of my left ear and I loved how my name rolled off his tongue.

A shudder ran through me. Yes, my underwear soaked with my juices. I dared not move and suspected I'd already given myself away. His sense of smell was highly acute— whichever animal he was. I clenched my ass cheeks, but it didn't help either; I still ached for his touch.

"Do you want me to touch you?" he asked near my right ear.

Curse him. I moved my face in that direction and felt his hot breath against my cheek.

Yes, I want you to touch and lick every inch of my body. I thought.

"Maybe," I said instead.

He chuckled, low and throaty.

"You're lying. Do you want my hands on your body?" Without waiting for a response, he placed his hands on my shoulders and they seared my skin. I felt heat beat against my back as he moved closer.

Oh gods, I could die right now.

"Maybe."

"You're lying."

I was a complete trembling mess. To want attention from him was uncouth, but he sent all my senses ablaze as if my body knew what it wanted while I was only the passenger.

Did I want him to touch me? *Hell, yes!*

"Your body responds to me, Ava," he whispered against the back of my neck and it sent all my hair to attention. Again he said my name in such a way it tightened my core. I shivered in anticipation.

His hands burned down my arms, then he gripped my ribs and rubbed the sides of my aching breasts. My core muscles clenched, and I whimpered.

"What if I moved my hands lower?"

Tyler moved his hands down the sides of my body in a painstakingly slow pace. My skin burned with desire. What I wanted him to do was rip off my clothing, fuck me with his fingers, then fuck me with his cock.

He pushed my legs apart, and a yelp escaped my lips. I lost balance and gripped his shoulders; it was an odd position and my shoulders strained as I held onto him with my arms behind my back. My ankle ached and stars flashed before my dark vision.

"Should I feel what's between your legs, Ava? I know

you have something I haven't seen before and I can smell your arousal, and you smell divine." He purred.

Oh gods. I was going to orgasm right here if he continued.

He stood back, giving me space. I exhaled and let go. He held onto my hips again to keep me from falling. I felt his chin on my shoulder and I leaned into him.

"How long has it been since anyone touched you?"

A year.

"A few weeks," I whispered.

"You're lying," he chuckled against my shoulder.

His right hand moved from my hip and slithered down the front of my body to the apex of my legs. I moaned and melted into him. I didn't want him to stop. He trailed his fingers down my shorts, under my panties until he found my slick folds. He grunted his pleasure at finding what he was looking for. He rubbed the swollen bud, sending a thousand volts through my body.

I couldn't believe this was happening. I wanted no one as much as I wanted him.

I moaned as he played with me and I rocked into his hand. I couldn't control my need as I sought release. I gasped when he shoved two fingers inside my heated sheath. He swore and pumped his fingers into me. His other hand snaked around the other side of my body and played with my pert nipple then the other, alternating between the two; ensuring each breast got the attention they deserved.

Tyler pumped his fingers inside me, sending me over, and I flexed around him. I gripped his powerful arm, feeling the corded muscles move beneath his skin. The orgasm hit me so hard the dark room spun and my legs gave out. Tyler caught me in his arms and I felt his rock hard body against my side.

"Do you want me to fuck you, Ava?"

"Gods yes."

I heard him smile.

"Finally, you're telling the truth," he said while kissing my forehead. He gently lay me on the bed and settled between my legs, removed the blindfold and hovered above me.

"Are you sure you want this?" He pushed his body against mine and I felt the hardness of his cock through his low-cut jeans.

I wanted this. I wanted all he offered; him, his body, his hard cock. I wanted it all. If this moment was the only time I had with him, I'd take it.

I stared up at his face, his kissable lips and I never wanted to kiss someone so badly and reached for him.

"Kiss me?"

It was the wrong thing to do.

He sat up as if I'd slapped him and shook his head.

"Get up," he ordered. "Forget it. Let me take you outside. I have stuff to do, anyway." He yanked on my left arm, I moaned but that didn't deter him. He tied the blind-fold tightly over my eyes and in one swift motion I was in his arms and out the door.

Chapter Twelve

AVA

I sat on the chair and stared off at nothing. I was dumbstruck at what had happened and how my body felt against his. I enjoyed how his hands burned against my skin, sending volts of sensual lightning throughout my body. And every time he neared, I couldn't think of anything else.

At least I was outside. I raised my chin like a flower and basked in the sun. The sounds of birds and insects calmed me, and the smell of the earth eased my busy mind, but not for long.

Instead of enjoying nature, the only thing on my mind was Tyler.

Tyler was very different compared to others I'd gone out with and even my ex. Although Tyler scared me he excited me; leaving me a trembling mess. And he frightened me in ways, the good thrilling kind, I'd never experienced before. But… There was always a but… If he went further than what had happened, was I just another notch on his jeans. I didn't want that. I'd promised myself the next guy would be different.

Then, what threw me completely off guard was what didn't happen. Knowing it was a mistake to try to kiss him. I'd never do it again. But was it a mistake to want him to touch me? Perhaps we were both in the wrong. In the end it was a good thing he didn't go any further because I wasn't thinking straight. He didn't want a girlfriend, only a girl-for-right-now.

I needed him to understand I'd never put him or his pack in harm's way, then he wouldn't have to blindfold me, and didn't have to touch me again. I didn't know which flavor were-animal they were, and I wasn't that type of person to hurt others. I'd been on the receiving end to know what not to do to others.

While he'd carried me, I'd tried explaining I wasn't here for them, but he ignored me. He'd stopped walking and set me down gently, it was very caring of him. I tried to say sorry about trying to kiss him and that I wouldn't do it again, but he had already left by the time I removed the blindfold.

A lump formed at the back of my throat, and I swallowed the tears. It was stupid to be so emotional. I felt bad and didn't know how to let him know I meant no harm. And I'd never touch his face again.

Tyler had placed my camera on the grass beside the chair and had left me at an area where I could see the river and the mountains; the view was magnificent, and I took a few landscape shots.

To get over what had transpired, I kept myself busy. I watched out for any insects, small animals or birds to take pictures. I'd even taken a few decent photos, all the while trying to ignore the voice at the back of my mind, but it was difficult.

Why did my body react to his? And so quickly? Why was I so emotional? A flurry of questions I had no answers to.

Then anger settled in. His reaction wasn't necessary. I crossed my arms and stared at the view. The rushing water didn't calm me like always. Tyler got me hot and bothered then dumped me like trash; I was overreacting, but still. It was rude. I wanted him and he just threw me away. That was his one and only chance at having any part of me. I wouldn't allow him near me again. It was pleasurable in his embrace, but never again.

I was still grumpy by the time the sky graced me with its bright colors at dusk. Nobody had checked up on me and I was hungry. From where I sat, the view of the mountain showed none of the huts, and I had no way of knowing which direction they were in. They had most likely built their huts between the trees and had made the roofs of branches as camouflage. The walk here was quick, which left me confused.

Perhaps leaving me here was on purpose and Tyler wanted me to leave, but I only had my camera bag. I needed my backpack to get home as my car keys were inside. And I hadn't had time to take any painkillers because he *distracted me.* I grumbled. The right side of my body throbbed and my stomach made strange gargling sounds.

"Are you ready?"

I jumped in the wooden chair, spinning around, knocking my knee against the armrest. I whimpered. I hit the armrest so hard a bump had already formed—another one to add to the collection.

"Yes, where have you been all day? I'm hungry."

"I was busy." Tyler approached with purpose. The shadows played against his face and naked chest. My heart raced at his sudden mood change. He ripped the material out of his jeans pocket and forcefully tied it over my eyes. "You need to stay in your hut tonight, do not come out. Do you understand?"

I nodded. "Yes," I whispered. My voice broke, feeling suddenly nervous again.

He handed me my camera, and I clutched it to my chest when he picked me up. The heat from his body was comforting, and I relaxed in his arms.

After a while, I cleared my throat to apologize again. "I didn't mean—"

"Shh."

"Get her out of the way. We need to finish," said another man I hadn't heard before. He sounded older and grumpier.

"Just give me five."

A door opened and hit the wall. Tyler stomped into the hut and dropped me on the bed. My ankle hit the side hard enough to draw a cry from me. He yanked off the blindfold so violently a piece of the material stung my cheek.

"Jeez, what's wrong with you? You don't have to hurt me," I moaned and tried to sit comfortably but no matter how I sat my body ached. On a table that wasn't there before, was a plate with meat, bread, and an apple. A bottle of water stood beside it. "Thanks for dinner," I mumbled.

He glowered down at me with conflict in his eyes. "Stay put," he warned again and exited, slamming the door shut.

I heard something tighten against the door, locking me inside.

Never mind, I didn't want to go anywhere, anyway. I didn't want to see their stupid clan or whatever they were doing. It was probably stupid anyway. All I wanted to do was eat, take painkillers, then sleep. I might shower, but I'd see if I had energy.

Chapter Thirteen

TYLER

I spent the entire day miserable.

When she lay beneath me, I stared at the delicate slope of her nose, her fair skin and wild, curly hair, I had to have her—not only her body but I felt the need to claim her. But then something stopped me. I couldn't continue until I knew for sure. Was it something she even wanted? Did she even want me that way? If I claimed her, would she want to live with me, here? It frustrated me, but that wasn't the primary reason.

After I'd left Ava at her secluded spot, I helped with preparations for the evening. Cheryl wordlessly slapped me then draped herself over Blaze, who shrugged. He knew the deal and besides; I wasn't the jealous type, and not over Cheryl—she was welcome to go for any guy who'd have her. And I'd accepted the slap—I deserved it, I really did. She was trying to make me jealous but I ignored them.

My mind raced as I chopped wood. Miles felled five trees and dragged them for me to chop into usable chunks for the fire tonight. With so many hikers over the weekend our fire would just be like any other campers fire.

Miles only glared at me. He knew better than to ask why I axed the wood with violence.

All I thought about was Ava. How her body reacted to mine, and I didn't do anything special to elicit that type of response.

And her smell, oh my gods—I was rock hard just thinking about her. And her warm slick slit begging for me to plunge into. But then the moment was ruined when she tried to kiss me. I overreacted, I should've just kissed her and every inch of her body, but then I stopped because my mind raced. I wanted to claim her lips and her body. My beast roared inside my head. He wanted her too.

And besides, Ash would've skinned me alive. She was not like our kind; she had no flavor animal to bond with; she was human.

I wanted to trust that she'd been hiking to take pictures of nature. My gut told me it was the truth, yet I needed to remain vigilant. We couldn't sacrifice the clan because of one female or how I thought I felt about her.

My mind ached from the confusion and I hated it. The axe smashed through the wood, splintering it.

"Easy." Miles dropped a felled tree. "What's got you so riled up?"

"Nothing." I glanced in the direction she was in, lifted the axe above my head and struck the wood, cutting a sizable chunk.

"Man, I've never seen you like this before. You like her don't you?"

"Shut up."

"I call it as I see it. You might be my future chieftain, but right now we're friends and I know your moods. You've never acted like this before. Why don't you claim her before you break the axe?"

"I can't. It would be pointless. Ash wouldn't approve."

"So what, ask for forgiveness afterwards."

I narrowed my eyes at Miles. He may be the runt of the litter, but he spoke wise words.

A low guttural sound came from the base of my throat.

Miles raised his hands. "I'm just saying. Claim her before someone else does. You know once the moon is above us someone will sniff her out, then you've lost your chance. And I guarantee you Claw will try his luck with her."

I stared at Miles for a heartbeat. Knowing Claw, he would. And if he knew I liked her, he'd do it just to spite me. I glanced in her direction again and my beast pushed to the surface.

"There's one last tree then you can go fetch her."

I doubted she'd run off, and didn't bother asking a youngling to watch over her. And after Miles had said that about Claw, I was glad I didn't—they wouldn't tell Claw everything about her.

When I neared the area, I leaned against a tree and watched her. She sighed and fisted her hands. Then she rubbed the bridge of her nose as if counting to ten.

I chuckled, it was mean to laugh at her expense, but I was glad I wasn't the only one having a bad day.

Unfortunately, the moment I remembered Ash's words, my anger flared just below the surface. He wanted her gone. He wanted nothing to do with humans. I should've asked

Windtalker how I should approach the issue with Ash. Perhaps he had a magic potion I could use.

And if Claw wanted to claim her, he would rip her apart shortly thereafter, like he did to his other play-things.

I needed to protect her. I needed her healed and gone. I couldn't claim her, I couldn't keep her here—she wouldn't be safe. I'd have to leave the clan, or I'd have to fight. The others might not accept her if I won, then what would I do?

It wasn't worth the risk; I'd rather remain alone than to risk her life.

Ash was a mean bastard, but Claw was evil.

I was still angry when I fetched Ava and ended up being a little rough with her. I felt bad but I had to. It was better for her if she hated me, but her body responded to mine which drove me crazy.

After I locked Ava in her hut, the sun had already started to set. My beast pushed to the surface, eager to run. *'Down Boy. You'll get your chance soon.'*

He sniffed the air—smelling the female.

'I want her, and I know you do, too,' Beast moaned in his saber voice inside my head. He rarely did that since I sensed his emotions and thoughts. We were part of the same being. It was only when he thought I was stubborn would he *speak* to me—like now.

'Ash would kill her. Claw will abuse her. We need to protect her by claiming her.'

I grunted, ignoring my saber voice.

'If anyone tries to stop you, you fight. We'll kill Ash. Then we'll kill Claw. You know you're better. Besides, Ash has had his time. It's

your turn to take over the clan. And you know, once you do, the clan will grow. We need fresh blood, and you're the one to get us there.'

'*I know..., I know...,*' I mumbled my thoughts, hoping to calm the saber down. He was right, but Ash was my father. I could kill Claw without thinking about it, but then Darla would be on my case along with Ash. They'd force me to leave and they might still go after Ava. I couldn't allow that.

"Tyler," Miles jogged toward me. "Ash wants you."

"Speak of the devil."

"What?"

"Nothing. Where is he?"

"His hut with his *mate*."

Darla was Ash's lover and Claws mother. She was nothing of mine. My mother had died giving birth to me and it didn't take Father long to find a replacement, but I'd never called her anything other than *Darla* and her bastard son was not my blood brother. She also had the squeakiest voice I'd ever heard—which meant she was utterly and completely annoying.

I found Ash sitting on the ground with Darla hanging on his back like a monkey. I didn't want to know what she was doing with her hands in his pants. I saw her naked flesh and cringed.

Something to the side caught my eye, and Claw sat against a tree. His gloomy gaze told me he was unhappy—and most likely plotting something. When things didn't go his way, he lashed out. And usually at my expense. And they never allowed me to fight back as hard as I wanted to.

I shot him one of my meanest stares to put him in his place. He flinched and averted his eyes. Just as I thought, he was still a whipped little boy trying to play with the big cats. Claw was only a year younger but very immature. And although he was nowhere near as strong as me, he was devious and evil. With each passing day he was giving in to his thirsty animal side, and losing more of his humanity. He was not only a danger to humans, but to our clan as well. He needed to be managed carefully.

"You wanted to see me?" I stood in such a way I couldn't see Darla's naked body.

"I'm giving the human two days, Tyler. She needs to leave first thing Monday morning before the humans exit the trails. It will be quieter. Do you understand? The others are complaining."

My brows furrowed. I shot daggers in Claw's direction, but he'd left. Nobody had mentioned anything to me. The 'others' Ash referred to, was most likely Darla or Claw—or both.

"What are they saying?"

"None of your business. I'm chieftain and they come to me with their problems."

That was code word for Darla had complained, she always had issues.

"I've heard others say they can smell her. The males will fight trying to get to the female. We can't have that."

Ah, there it was... Claw had been sniffing the air; wanting a taste. After his last girlfriend, Darla had forbidden him from looking at another woman, never mind touching them.

I twisted my body to see where he was. Miles stood guard outside Ava's hut and some tension eased. But I needed to find Claw. If our numbers weren't small, I'd have had him killed long ago. But things could change tonight.

"And it's the full moon." Ash glanced up through his bushy eyebrows.

"I heard you the first time. She has her stuff and her medication. In two days I'll take her back." Perhaps I needed to get her out of here tonight before the full moon festivities began. This was a silent warning I couldn't ignore.

As if sensing my thoughts, Ash added. "There isn't a way around the trails without the humans seeing you. And it's the weekend, all the trails are busy, if you leave now they will see you. Even at night. And there's no way you can go through the leopard's territory. They will kill you."

"Fine, I won't go now." He was right. We couldn't leave now, even though I wanted to.

He grunted and kissed Darla's cheek. He shooed me away, and I rolled my eyes when my back was to them.

Claw was hiding somewhere. I walked past the tree he always sat under and found broken pieces of a branch caked with dried blood. I walked the outer perimeter of our hidden village and couldn't pick up his scent.

Once back inside the village, Miles remained outside Ava's hut and I nodded at him.

I called Blaze over to assist me with a few things for the feast.

As the chieftain's son, I needed to fulfill a role which included the full moon feasts, assist those young fledglings who were yet to change into their sabers, and ensure everyone's safety within the village.

When we'd arrived two years ago, we found a spot on the mountain with flat ground and hidden within the tall trees and thick vegetation. We'd built our huts between the trees and ensured nobody saw our village from the sky, or the hiking trails. We had roughly thirty small huts scattered in the vast area, with two sabers circling the perimeter hourly.

Ash still hadn't found out about the deer mauled by someone. And if my suspicions were correct, it was Claw.

Even though I was busy, my thoughts drifted to Ava. No matter what I thought was right, my heart wanted her. My beast wanted her.

I should've kissed her, but when her hand reached for my cheek so tenderly, I recoiled. Perhaps I wasn't used to someone so breakable and fragile wanting me. The way she reached out for me with that look in her eyes told me she wanted more than just my body, even if she didn't know it herself. I wanted to make her mine. I should just claim her and ask for forgiveness afterward.

———

By eleven o'clock Miles had said he'd heard her move around, then finally settled down. It eased my nerves. I hoped she slept through it all.

When the moon's power struck at its highest, those who were younger couldn't control their saber and shifted into their beasts. They grunted and groaned, followed by hissing and clawing of trees. They wanted to hunt. They wanted to kill; they wanted the taste of blood and flesh.

I glanced at her hut and hoped she was asleep. The last thing we needed was a human distraction. I was grateful I couldn't smell her as I stood outside the hut, which meant none of the other males could either.

The lock was still in place—I the only one holding the key.

Windtalker came out of nowhere and latched onto my arm.

"Have you felt it yet, son?" he said in his quiet, calm voice.

"What are you talking about?" I feigned ignorance and smiled slyly. I had felt it, like a jolt into my sternum; I couldn't miss it.

"You know." He glanced at me, narrowing his good eye. He patted my forearm. "The girl, you idiot. How does your chest feel whenever you are near her?" He slapped my chest. "Does she make you feel any different? I know you feel it foolish boy."

I glanced at the hut. "I have," I smiled at him. "I have an overwhelming need to protect her."

He nodded his understanding. "And you've never felt that way over anyone before?" He let go of my arm. "Open your heart to her, Tyler, and you'll see much more than meets the eye."

I pictured the way her body responded to mine and in a way no other had before.

"Trust me, she's the one for you. I can feel it," he said. "And don't worry about Ash," he mumbled cryptically and continued walking in the river's direction.

My beast wanted her, and so did I.

My beast rippled beneath my skin, and I didn't hold him back. I arched my back and roared. My joints pulled and twisted. My fur spread over my skin and my beast was out; and he was hungry. He sniffed the air. Claw emerged in his smaller, yet bulkier saber and stared at me. His bright yellow eyes darted to the hut and back to me. He wanted to go there—he wanted to hurt Ava. I saw the warning in his eyes.

We couldn't allow it to happen and would fight him if he went anywhere near her.

We hissed and roared at him, sending him away with his tail between his legs.

My beast headed toward her hut, I tried to pull him

away but he wouldn't listen. His vision tunneled, and we moved forward. We wanted her. Now.

He sniffed under the door, and she moved off the bed.

When in this form his/my vision was darker while the brights were brighter, our sense of smell and hearing superb. I smelled her while my saber made that rasping, coughing sound. We hissed when another saber neared, but my warning was enough to deter him. I lifted my leg and pissed against the door. My scent stained the wood, and I growled my satisfaction.

She gasped and jumped back onto the bed when my urine seeped under the door.

Now I was hungry.

Chapter Fourteen

AVA

When the beast hissed and growled outside my door, I suspected it might be Tyler. Then when he'd marked his territory, I knew it was definitely him. I smiled, although mildly disgusted. I didn't know what his plans were, but he'd already staked his claim and almost bit into another male who'd neared. The overwhelming stench of urine left me sick to my stomach; I was just glad my dinner hadn't repeated on me.

From the calls, roars, and growls from the pack, I surmised they were tigers or lions. Although I'd never heard of a pack hiding on the outskirts of Sterling Meadow and in the forest reserved for humans. They couldn't have been leopards, as they already had their own territory in one part of the forest, and so I doubted they were rogue leopards. I'd heard the leap in Sterling Meadow was one of the best, and there was already an established pride of lions. If I thought about it, it was possible they were a streak of tigers, or even ligers.

That could be why they didn't want anyone to know

they were here. I hadn't heard of many streaks of ligers. But then again, it didn't sound like they enjoyed the company of humans.

Whatever the reason, I would not provoke them and would gladly keep to myself.

Grateful they separated me from the outside while they did their thing. I stayed in the hut and responded to Derek's text messages. I didn't mention what had happened; I didn't want him getting on his high horse rescuing me. It was none of his business.

I washed in the small shower; it was one of those portable camping types I used on longer camping trips. The water was warm, and I'd cleaned the dirt off my body, changed into clean underwear and clothing. My ankle still ached even after rubbing ointment everywhere and taking two painkillers.

I was in desperate need of sleep, but the raucous feast outside kept me from my slumber. It was only after the third painkiller did Mr. Sandman steal me away.

Scratching against wood brought me out of my dream; whatever it was, I couldn't remember, anyway. I blinked rapidly as I took in the room's darkness. Dark shadows played in every corner, with no light from the silver moon, nor a light from outside. The feast was no longer happening, and the silence filled the night.

The bed moved, and I held my breath. A low, raspy cough left me cold and too numb to move. When I found the confidence, I slowly turned in the sound's direction. A cloud moved bathing the hut in silver moonlight. I saw the front paws of an enormous cat perched at the end of the bed with its hind legs on the ground. He was a mountain of a kitty; his intense green/yellow eyes staring at me, into me and piercing my soul. I moved my arm and touched his closest paw; soft and fluffy with dangerous claws.

"Tyler?" I reached for his face. I didn't know if it was him, but I doubted any other would dare try.

He growled, and I pulled back my hand.

The cat climbed off. I reached for the oil lamp beside me. The moment bright light touched the hut, the cat hissed. I stared in wonder at the marvel of a beast. I had been completely wrong. He wasn't a liger nor a tiger. He was absolutely beautiful with his elongated canine teeth, stunningly deadly.

I sat up, throwing off the blanket as heat swirled around me.

My heart raced as I took in his size.

"Tyler?" I reached again.

He neared and pressed his enormous head against my hand. I scratched his cheek, then behind his ear, and he purred.

I cupped his massive head in my hands and pressed my head against his. He smelled like earth, animal, and raw meat.

When I pulled away, the giant saber-tooth morphed into the honed man. Tyler stood before me, his chest rising and falling, his yellow eyes glowing. He was beautiful.

He stood tall and imposing. His body a work of art, every muscle defined, and I ached to touch every curve. I raked my eyes over his body and heat pooled between my legs. A soft whimper escaped my lips, eliciting a sly smile on Tyler's face, highlighting his sharp jaw and heavenly features.

For some strange, unknown reason, he attracted me like

no other, my entire body wanted him. I thought of him adding me to his list of women he had his way with, and I actually resigned to the notion that it was just a one-night fling. Who cared if he was using me? Perhaps I was using him, too. I'd get rid of my frustration, forget about the crappy men I'd had before and I'd use his body and then I'd get on with my life. I could handle that. That's all this was, anyway.

Tyler approached with purpose and all my thoughts evaporated into thin air.

All I thought of was him.

He reached for my top, and I allowed him to remove it. He helped me to stand. He stood so close and with nowhere to go I pressed up against his hard body, his erection digging into my stomach and without thinking I grabbed his cock as he pulled down my shorts. He stilled and waited; I had him where I wanted him and lowered my face until my lips surrounded him and I sucked teasingly. I licked up his shaft, forcing him to groan in pleasure. I smiled. I took him in my mouth going as far down as I could handle. When he reached the back of my throat, he grabbed my hair and kept me in position. My eyes watered as my tongue played with him and my hand squeezed gently.

"Ava?" he moaned my name, filled with unspoken meaning, and I wanted to please him.

I came up and licked around the tip and tasted him; slightly salty and musky. It was his taste, and I enjoyed it. I continued moving down and up his shaft, licking and sucking.

"Stop, or I'm fucking your face." He pulled me off him and motioned me to lie on the bed.

He kissed the nape of my neck and worked his way down my body. His tongue teased my nipple, he sucked and nibbled before moving on to the next one. He kissed my stomach and nibbled my hip bone. My hands mussed his hair and when he found what he was looking for, I pulled. His tongue parted my moist folds and darted inside my heat. His purr vibrated against my pert bud, sending a wave of sensual energy throughout my body. I bucked beneath him, my hands still in his hair, keeping him between my legs. He chuckled and continued licking and sucking.

"You taste just like I imagined." His dark gaze raked up my body and all I could do was smile. When he continued licking and sucking, my eyes rolled back into my head. I could die right now.

He teased a finger near my opening and I gasped when he entered; he grunted, pulled his finger out and in a second hovered above me.

"I don't want to wait anymore." He lowered himself on to me. "I should've done this earlier," he said and kissed me. His soft lips were gentle against mine, his tongue teasing me to open for him, and I did. We kissed with passion and a deeper need that went beyond our bodies. And I loved it, I wanted more.

He broke our kiss and worked his way down my neck with soft kisses with his lips, making my arms pebble in delight.

I wrapped my legs around his waist and rocked into him, wanting more, eagerly needing.

"Be patient," he said teasingly.

With one hand, he positioned himself near my opening and slowly eased the tip inside. When I moaned, he pulled out. I cursed. I opened my mouth to say something else when he thrusted slowly, forcing a gasp from my lips. He groaned low in the back of his throat as he backed out, but before leaving completely he eased inside, filling every part of me. Slowly he inched out, then thrusted back in until he found his rhythm; skin slapping skin filled the silence.

He licked my neck as he crushed me to the bed, pumping in long deep strokes. He claimed every part of me with every powerful thrust, both lost to the passion as lust consumed us. He brought me to the edge then slowly backed down, leaving me wanting more, needing more, needing him.

I rocked into him, meeting him half-way with each deep thrust as I sought release. My back arched as the helpless desire crushed into me. I lowered my hand, but he pushed it away, replacing with his hand instead. He thrust slowly and purposely, rubbing my clit with his hand, pushing me over the edge. My head spinning, my vision tunneled as the orgasm smashed into me and I flexed around him.

Tyler maintained his rhythm as each deep plunge had him grunting with sweat peppering his face. With each thrust of his cock, my nails dug into his back and I writhed beneath him.

His hips jerked and his thrusts became uncoordinated. His cock throbbed and pulsed as he pumped his hot seed into me, sending me over the edge with him.

My thighs trembled, sweat glistened off our bodies as I clung to him. I was thoroughly fucked and exhausted.

Slowly he slid out, his cock still large even when flaccid.

We shared no words. Our actions spoke for us. Tyler pulled me into the curve of his body, kissed my neck and I relaxed in his embrace. For the first time in a long time, I felt comfortable and secure.

Chapter Fifteen

TYLER

She felt so warm in my arms it hurt letting go. I needed to secure the perimeter of the village like I did every morning. But with her in my arms, I struggled.

Afterwards I pulled her into the front of my body and fell asleep. Last night was the first time I'd slept longer than just a couple of hours.

Even my lazy saber stretched and yawned like he had all morning to wake up. He liked our female and loved what we did to her body last night. My cock stiffened thinking about her. I'd love to ravage her again, but she seemed so peaceful. We had time.

I kissed her cheek, and she stirred, pulling my arm closer to her. I nestled into her neck, my front pressed against her back, and she fit perfectly against me; as if made only for me.

I was a stubborn fool. I kept thinking about what Ash wanted for the clan instead of what I wanted—and I wanted Ava. Yes, she was human, yes she was fragile, but she had me to protect her. I could only hope she wanted me as much.

Chapter Sixteen

AVA

I stretched lazily and smiled. I felt rejuvenated, not remembering the last time I'd slept so well. My eyes flitted open when I realized I was the only one in bed. I sat up and scanned the room; he'd left sometime during the morning.

A cool breeze caressed my naked skin. I pulled the blanket tighter over my body, remembering I'd fallen asleep in his arms with only his body keeping me warm. My smile stretched wider and my cheeks heated as butterflies fluttered in my core. I felt like a schoolgirl with a crush. I was thirty-something, only had one serious boyfriend who had almost killed me, and to think I'd vowed never to love again so soon. But this wasn't love—it was something else. It was far too soon for love, wasn't it?

Then, my usual thought process began; when something went well, it was bound to explode and end badly. I wondered how he'd react to me during the day, if at all. Last night was just a one-night stand, and I expected nothing else. It was safer that way. To protect what's left of my scarred heart, I wouldn't dream of anything else. It was just a onetime thing, nothing more.

Once dressed, I sent Derek a text message letting him know I'd be staying for a few more days. I couldn't leave yet; my ankle still ached and doubted I could walk a mile on it. And I didn't want him to worry come tomorrow morning when I didn't show up at work with the pictures I'd promised.

A soft knock on the door brought me out of my thoughts. Before I answered the door it opened. It wasn't Tyler.

"Morning." Miles entered with a plate of food; bread, meat, and an apple. "How are you feeling?"

I smiled. "Good, how was the festivities last night."

Miles froze and stared with wide green eyes. "What did you hear?"

"Don't worry so much. Your secrets are safe with me." I winked and took the plate from him. I started picking at the meat. "Where's Tyler?"

"Busy, he asked me to drop this off quickly." He twitched nervously.

I frowned. "What's wrong?"

"Nothing." Miles left before I responded and locked the door behind him.

Not knowing what that was about, I ignored it and enjoyed breakfast.

My phone lit up with messages from Derek.

'Did something happen?', 'Are you okay?' and *'Do you need me to bring a rescue?'*

I rolled my eyes and started texting back, *"I'm fi—"*

when the door opened and Tyler stood in the doorjamb, cocked his head to the side and scowled.

"What are you doing?" His mouth twitched. I didn't like his expression.

"What? This?" I raised my phone. "I'm just letting my boss know I'm okay?"

"Why?"

"I'm here on assignment—"

"Show me."

I offered him my phone, which he grabbed and read.

"My people are at risk if anyone else knows about us. Please," — he handed back my phone, — "we can't risk it."

"I know, let me send the message and then I'm all yours." My cheeks heated, and I glanced up at him. "I mean… let me just put this man's mind at ease. If I don't calm him down, he will send someone to look for me, or he'd come himself."

I quickly finished the text, ensuring it had sent before plugging it into my portable charger.

I ate the last morsel of meat, grabbed my camera bag, added my first aid kit and stood.

Tyler produced the blindfold from his pocket and my heart skipped a beat, thinking of yesterday and how my body reacted to his slight touch. A sly smile stretched across his face as he stared at me. He pointed to the centre of the room. I nodded my understanding and stepped toward him, glancing up. I sucked in air, breathing in his scent. Flashes of him on top of me last night heated my neck. I fidgeted with my camera bag and closed my eyes.

I felt him move behind me, curling his fingers around my neck and moved my head to one side. Soft lips touched my skin, burning the spot. I leaned back, one hand grabbed my waist and he pulled me closer. He licked up my neck then behind my ear, sending a cascade of goosebumps everywhere.

"I love how your body responds to my touch."

"Uh-huh." I couldn't concentrate on anything but his lips and hands on my body. At least his actions answered my question about how he'd react to me when he saw me this morning.

A low guttural moan came from the base of his throat. I whimpered in delight. He was tender yet firm. He was everything I didn't know I wanted. And in the back of my mind I thought that perhaps it wasn't a onetime thing after all.

"I need to go," he whispered near my ear. "I need to take care of a few things today. Miles will watch over you. Try not to get hurt," he chuckled and tied the blindfold.

Chapter Seventeen

AVA

Tyler left me at a different spot but the same chair waited for me, only this time it was closer to the river. The scenery was beautiful as I snapped a few landscape shots, woodpeckers, Monarch butterflies, and a wildcat.

Tyler had left a bottle of water which I'd already finished. I used the bathroom and dressed my wounds. My ankle still throbbed but the swelling had gone down, and I took two painkillers. I should be able to walk unaided tomorrow.

When Miles hadn't arrived by lunch time an uneasiness settled in my bones. Tyler had said Miles would arrive shortly after I arrived, but he hadn't.

I had no way of knowing which direction to go back and had to wait.

Twigs snapped in the distance and I spun around, narrowing my eyes at something moving near the trees. Unsure of the animal and therefore whether to be loud or remain quiet; I hid behind the chair and waited.

Whichever animal it was, it hadn't revealed itself. It had

most likely left, and the tension between my shoulders relaxed. I stood, turned around to take a picture of the river when something big caught my eye. A saber stalked. Its bright blue eyes trained on me. I froze. It had different markings on its body. And Tyler had yellow eyes when he was in his beast. This was another saber.

"Miles?"

The saber shook its head, understanding me.

"Who are you?"

It made a rasping sound, hissed and closed the gap. I backed up, colliding with the chair and climbed over it. The saber pounced, landed on the chair and hissed at me through the bars.

"I don't like you," it said through its large jaw but I understood the warning.

I glanced at its magnificent body and frowned.

"Are you the girl I saw with Tyler two nights ago?"

If this was the same woman I'd seen having sex with Tyler, then she had reason to be pissed. But Tyler had said she wasn't his girlfriend, and I wondered whether they had an open relationship—if so, why was she stalking me?

She roared and jumped over the chair, landing softly on her paws.

"Why are you doing this?" I put my camera bag between us; doubtful it would protect me from her, but I had to try something. As much as I didn't want to hurt her, if she attacked, I would do everything to protect myself.

"What's going on?" Miles nursed a head wound. "Get back, Darla. I won't tell Ash what happened if you back away. Now!"

My eyes flitted from Miles to *Darla*, but she kept her dark gaze on me.

"Darla! If you attack her, it forces Tyler to fight Ash. You know that would be bad."

Darla hissed and retreated. She bared her sharp teeth, another warning, and dashed into the forest behind her.

"I think I wet myself." I laughed nervously and glanced down. My pants felt wet, but I didn't piss myself completely.

"Are you okay?"

"No… yes… I don't know. She scared the bejeezus out of me. Are you okay?" I placed my camera bag on the chair and picked up my first aid kit. "You're bleeding."

"Don't worry about me, I'll heal just fine." He lowered my hand when I wanted to touch the gash in his forehead.

"Did she do this to you?"

He nodded and glanced over his shoulder in the direction Darla had gone.

"Is she the one I saw having sex with Tyler?"

"No."

"Why then? I don't even know her."

Miles cleared his throat. "She's our chieftain's lover."

"Okay, but that doesn't explain why she wanted to rip out my throat."

"It's not my place to tell you. Tyler can."

"I'll do what?" Boomed his voice from somewhere in the forest. Tyler emerged, chest heaving as if he sprinted here. "What's going on?"

Miles shot me a warning glance before turning around. "There was a misunderstanding—"

"Did she do that to you?"

Miles glanced over his shoulder with pleading eyes. I didn't know what was going on, who Ash and Darla were, or why she attacked me. What puzzled me the most was why Tyler would fight Ash. But I wouldn't say anything, especially after the look I got from Miles.

"It was an accident." I raised my camera bag. "He gave me a fright."

Tyler smirked and slapped Mile's shoulder. "You can head back so long," Tyler said to Miles while he stared at me.

Miles nodded and headed back.

Tyler's glare sent a shiver down my spine, striking my core. His hungry eyes stared at me as if I alone made everything worthwhile. He literally took my breath away as I struggled for air. Heat rose within me and if I hadn't injured my ankle, I'd run to him, wrap my legs around him and have my way with him; Miles watching or not.

"What are you thinking about?" He took my camera bag and placed it gently on the ground. "And I'll know if you lie," he said with a twinkle in his eye.

His warning spoke of carnal promises; if I told him what I wanted to do to him would he allow it, but if I lied, he'd have his way with me. I guessed either way he'd be leaving me breathless and wanting more.

I smiled up at him, his heat beating against my chest. From the expression he wore I surmised he enjoyed last night as much as I did.

My breathing labored as our eyes met, the connection sealed.

"What I wanted to do if I wasn't in pain." I glanced at my swollen ankle.

He pressed his index finger under my chin and raised my face so I looked in his eyes.

"You don't need to catch me, Ava, I'll lie right here for you to do as you please," he whispered gruffly, pressed his lips against my cheek. He moved down to my neck, his lips hovering there, waiting. I felt his hot breath against my chilled skin, leaving me shivering.

I wrapped my arms around his neck, rocked onto my toes and winced when pain shot up my leg. He picked me up, and I wrapped my legs around his waist. He sat on the chair while I straddled him. His jeans buckle pressed painfully against me, I undid it and zipped him free.

Ripe with excitement, I knew I wouldn't last long. I climbed off and slowly slipped out of my shorts and panties; giving him a twirl. Once naked, I stalked him without hurting myself, which made him smile. His dark gaze caressed my body as if his hands were on me and I knew then that's all I wanted; *him*.

I hadn't wanted to be with anyone as much as I did with Tyler. We'd only known each other a few days, yet I felt at peace and at home whenever I was near him. I wanted to make him happy, as I knew he'd make me happy.

Tyler pulled his jeans down to his ankles, and his cock stood at attention, waiting. I placed my left knee beside his thigh first, then my right knee next to his other thigh while my hand rubbed up and down his steel shaft. He slid down slightly in the chair to get comfortable and his rock hard cock throbbed in my hand.

He reached for the apex of my legs, rubbed my moist folds, and hummed when he licked his fingers.

"I can't get enough of your taste."

I blushed. Then slowly, teasingly, I lowered myself onto him. He grunted when I sat up and right before he slipped out, I slowly sat down again. I gave him some of his own medicine and did this a few times, slowly, riding his cock up and down, coating his shaft with my juices.

He gripped my hips, controlling my movements and pumped hard, deep thrusts into me.

I clutched his neck while my legs strained, hovering over him. His lips twitched into a smile. Sweat peppered his face, and he pulled me to his body. He kissed down my neck, and all I thought of was his hands on my body while riding his cock. He stretched me wide and deep as he drove into me, filling me.

Tyler grunted in animal-like fervor when I pushed my palms into his chest and shifted my hips, grinding my pussy in a circular motion, maintaining a delicious rhythm. My core tightened and contracted around him. I screamed his name. He threw his head back, letting out a low groan. I continued rocking in slow movements when his cock throbbed, filling me with his hot seed. In a wave of paradox sensations, chills shot up my spine as my fiery heat engulfed him.

I collapsed against his chest, spent and hot.

His heart thundered in his chest, beating against my own. He wrapped his arms around me, gently kissing the top of my head.

His cock twitched within me, sending another flurry of electricity through my core.

"Feel like going for a dip in the river?"

Chapter Eighteen

TYLER

I dived under the water and came up behind Ava, forcing a scream from her lips.

"You gave me a fright," she said, slapping my shoulder. She couldn't stay angry for long and burst out laughing as she clung to my neck. "Tell me about yourself." She leaned forward, her sensual lips locking onto mine. Her face was so much smaller than mine, delicate and beautiful. Her lips were just the right plumpness and soft. I could kiss her all day.

"What do you want to know?"

"Duh! Everything. When did you get here? Do you work or live off the land? I want to know it all."

I told her someone had sold our land, the new owner had even showed us the title deed he'd purchased, and they transferred the money to an untraceable offshore bank account. My father didn't know what was happening until they showed up chasing us from the land. He was the only one who knew where the title deed was kept. He claimed they had stolen it, had changed the information and sold the land as if it were theirs. When the developer brought bulldozers to our land, we had to leave or risk arrest and exposure of our kind.

This was another reason Ash hated humans, but I didn't tell her this. I didn't want her fearing him, or the clan.

I explained how we traveled aimlessly in search of a place to live and remain hidden, but it was difficult since most of the land had humans occupying them. We eventually came across this forest and stayed. We'd been here for over two years and hadn't crossed paths with other were-animals, or humans. Until Friday.

Ava smiled sheepishly and pulled me closer.

"I'm sorry, I really am. But not sorry at the same time. I'm glad I met you." Her honey-colored eyes shone golden in the sunlight. Her pale skin glowed and her smile was contagious.

"To be honest, I've been thinking about that," — I squeezed her waist, — "and I'm glad you watched me have sex with another woman. Did you enjoy it?"

She slapped me playfully. "Pig!" Her cheeks glowed a healthy shade of pink.

She may have said I was a pig, but I saw the twinkle in her mischievous eyes when I asked if she enjoyed watching. I saw in her expression as she remembered that evening, and brushed my thumb against her cheek.

"You still haven't told me what you do."

I wanted to curl my lips in disdain, not for her but the question. I hated explaining what I did for a living. I always got mixed comments ranging from *'that's outstanding'* to *'you're a pig'*. I ripped off the proverbial bandaid and told her.

"I'm a financial consultant and trader."

"Oh, okay, that's not so bad. Do you have many clients?"

Ava may have said it wasn't so bad, but I saw the flicker of contempt cross her face before she asked her next question. Everyone had their own opinion on financial traders. Some were unscrupulous and deserved to be strung up by their necks, but I wasn't like them.

"I have my own business, and my clients are well off. My client lists consist mostly of vampires and they have old money and I help them build their businesses in today's markets. And I do everything online."

She stared with glazed over eyes, blinked, then asked. "This is going to sound terrible and sorry for asking, but are you rich?"

I grinned. The question was bound to come up, eventually.

"Let's just say my great grandchildren will want for nothing. And if invested wisely, neither would their kids."

"Just so you know, I'm not a gold digger." She started letting go, but I pulled her closer. It was as if she thought by just holding on to me, I'd think those were her intentions. "So does that mean you could buy any land you want?"

I nodded. "I could and I looked. But there wasn't anything big enough at the time, and it would mean revealing ourselves; and right now, under Ash's leadership, we're staying put. But when things change, who knows what would happen." I smiled reassuringly and nipped at her jawline. I meant what I said. If I became chieftain things would change and I might move us out of the shadows. There was an entire world to discover and nothing to be afraid of anymore.

Ava told me about herself. She grew up on a farm in Illinois, named all their farm animals to keep her dad from slaughtering or selling them. How she loved animals and wanted to work for National Geographic. She had a wonderful childhood even though they were not wealthy, but her parents loved her and that's what counted most. When she told me her parents had died in a car accident, her eyes misted.

I asked whether she'd had any serious boyfriends, and she replied only one. When she relayed how he'd almost killed her, my blood boiled. I wanted to know everything about this useless piece of shit to rid the earth of his corpse.

"Calm down, Tyler, please." She planted soft kisses over my cheek. "He is worthless and doesn't deserve another thought. Please, forget I said anything."

An overwhelming sense came over me; that I wanted to protect her and harm those who had hurt her. My feelings for Ava were different to what I felt for Cheryl. I didn't understand them, but I liked how it made me feel. I liked to have purpose, and she gave that to me.

"You know I can't, Ava—"

"But you must. Only if he comes after me again, do you have my permission to do with him as you please. He deserves no more of my attention. Until that day happens, can we forget about him and only concentrate on *us*?" The word slipped out, and she gasped, realizing her assumption. I smiled at her, which made her smile, and it brightened her face. She recovered quickly by adding. "I really don't want to waste time speaking about him. I want to know more about you."

"You can't possibly know everything about me in an hour."

"I know that," — she bit her lip, — "I like you, Tyler. At first I wasn't expecting much, didn't want to, but... I want to see more of you, you know? If you want to see more of me?" She shrugged; the genuine question hung silently on her lips. She struggled to get the words out, and I thought I'd help.

"Are you asking me to be your boyfriend?" I smirked.

"We're not in grade school."

I laughed, which prompted her to join me.

Did I want this? Did I really want this human female? I enjoyed her company, the way she spoke about animals and how she preferred to sit among nature.

Since I found her Friday night, she had been all I thought about. She clouded my mind and filled me with hope. My stomach ached when I wasn't near her, and my chest fluttered when I was. The confusion of it all only settled once she was in my arms.

It left me frustrated, irritated, and confused; *she was human*. Other shifters had human mates before, and this would be no different. But did she want me as her mate? It was meant to be forever and not something I could just blurt out and ask; I needed to wait until the chance presented itself. It may be too soon and I didn't want to scare her away. Besides, I wanted to know more about her first. And if we were to spend more time together, I couldn't have her blindfolded. She needed to see my world to decide for herself. To decide whether she wanted to be with me, here.

"I'd like nothing more than to be your boyfriend." I kissed her temple, pulled her closer against me and felt her heart racing against my chest.

Once dressed, I didn't see the need to blindfold Ava. She had expressed her desires to continue seeing me, meaning she'd need to know everything about me and the rest of the sabers. And to do that, she needed to see us.

I needed to speak to Ash about this. I didn't need the clan's blessing for the partner I chose but I needed to inform Ash; Ava was human, and she'd be sticking around for much longer. I'd have to make Ash accept this somehow. I wanted her to feel comfortable around the other sabers and not have to blindfold her every time. I wanted to show her my world, and she needed to see it all.

"Oh, my!" Ava said as we neared the huts. She opted to walk on her own, using me as a walking aid, and we traversed at a slow pace. "There are so many. No wonder I couldn't find any when I looked. You camouflage your huts well. Which one is yours?"

"You're sleeping in mine. I'm bunking with Miles at the moment."

"Well, you can always bunk with me," she said, batting her eyelashes.

"I just might." An uneasiness settled between my shoulder blades, and I stopped us from walking any farther. The hairs on my forearms rose. I didn't like it. "Hey, listen, can I blindfold you and carry you to your hut. I need to speak with Ash before I bring you out of the closet as my girlfriend... so to speak."

"Sure," she giggled as I tied the material around her head, covering her eyes.

Once Ava was safely in the hut, I locked the door, pocketing the key. I called Miles over, who had healed from his head wound. I didn't like how he and Ava had lied to me—I'd seen Darla slink back to the clan and I'd known she was up to something; her and Claw. Then when I saw Mile's cut on his head, I knew Darla had done it. And I knew Darla wanted to hurt Ava.

"Where's Claw and Darla?"

Miles nervously scanned the area. "I don't know. Your dad is looking for them too."

"Where is Ash?"

"He's gone back to his hut. He's sent five males to look for them and is waiting for her at his hut. He's pissed."

I hated speaking with Ash when he was in a mood, but this couldn't wait. I needed him to know about Ava, and the sooner the better.

"Stay here. I don't want either of those two coming near Ava. I'm telling Dad I'm claiming her."

A broad smile stretched across Mile's face. "You, dog, you. Go!"

A storm of emotions swirled around Ash; he paced in front of his hut, deep in thought.

"Father, can we speak?"

"Not now, Tyler, can't you see I'm busy."

"Yeah, I noticed," I said with sarcasm laced in my words. "It's important." I didn't bother waiting for his reply. I stood in his way so he didn't have an excuse to ignore me. Before the words escaped me, he pushed me out of the way. My beast roared, forcing a growl from my lips, and I pushed him back. Ash punched me in the face, and I elbowed him.

That day I'd been dreading had finally arrived, forcing my hand. I would kill him if he pushed me too far.

"Stop, I'm trying to talk with you."

He didn't stop. He launched in the air; I backed away from him, the moment he landed I kicked his hip and he fell to the ground with a grunt.

"Stop," I pleaded. "I don't want to hurt you."

"You can't hurt me."

Ash was taking his frustrations out on me, instead of Darla. I wondered what he'd found out about her.

Ash charged, raising his fists and swung. I side stepped, punching him in the jaw. His head knocked sideways, something crunched, and he collapsed to the ground. He moaned, unmoving.

"Christ, I didn't want to fight you." I gripped him under his arms and pulled him near his hut. "What I wanted to tell you before this pissing contest is, I'm claiming Ava. The right thing to do was inform you before you heard it from someone else."

Ash narrowed his dark green eyes, and I expected a flurry of cuss words, but he said nothing. He exhaled deeply and wiped blood from his mouth. He nodded, his eyes misted, and swallowed hard; his Adam's apple bobbing up and down.

My shoulders dropped, and I relaxed my shoulders. I expected him to fight again, but he said and did nothing.

He hung his head, then finally glanced up with tears in his eyes. "Your mother said you would fall for a human. I didn't want to believe you were as weak as me," — he nervously glanced around whether anyone else heard, — "she said you would be like me."

My brows furrowed.

Ash nodded. "Your mother was human, Tyler." He raised his arms, and I pulled him to his feet. He kept hold of my upper arms. "She died giving birth to you—"

"Oh shame, is daddy-dearest telling the sad, sad story."

I ignored Darla's remark. She was trying to provoke me.

"Where have you been?" Ash asked Darla. His tone sent a chill to my bones.

"I told you I was going for a walk."

"She's lying. She attacked Miles and Ava earlier."

Darla turned her vicious glare my way, but it did nothing. I closed the distance between us and glowered down at her.

"I've never liked you, Darla. Stay away from my mate and my friend."

"Your mate?" she said through a sarcastic laugh while glancing at Ash, confirming whether it was true.

Ash nodded.

"Well, well, well. It seems the apple doesn't fall far from the tree." She glared daggers at Ash, then snaked her arm around his waist. "Let's go inside—"

"Did you attack them?" Ash gently unhooked her fingers from his body and kept her at arm's length.

"I was hungry and went hunting. It's not my fault she's in the wrong place at the right time. It must be her human stench." Her eyes flitted in my direction.

"We don't attack our own, Darla. You know this."

"She isn't like us. And besides, it was an accident." She walked past Ash and entered the hut. "I'm lying down. Call me if there's any excitement."

I didn't appreciate her attitude, and from my father's expression, neither did he.

"Where is your son?" I called after her. I had to tell Ash about Claw. When Darla didn't answer, I said in a low voice Darla couldn't hear. "Claw is killing animals again, and I'm concerned he might go for Ava."

Soul piercing screams filled the air, and I knew it was too late.

Chapter Nineteen

TYLER

Running toward Ava's hut, I found Miles lying unconscious on the ground with his head bleeding. I blasted through the door, ripping it off its hinges, but the hut was empty. There's blood on the floor, her camera smashed, and a piece of her clothing soaking in blood.

Panic settled in and for the first time in my life, I was scared. My chest ached at the thought of losing her. I needed her by my side, and wouldn't stop until I found her, and when I did, I'd kiss every inch of her body. My saber wanted her, but I wanted her more. We had to find her. And we'd kill to get her back.

My saber rippled through my body; he was furious. Claw had taken our mate. I didn't have time to stop him. He smashed through me and roared loudly, ensuring Claw heard. I stretched my saber body as I readied to hunt Claw. My sense of smell was better in my beast, and I would ensure Claw got what he deserved.

Ash dashed into the hut with wide eyes upon hearing my call and shook his head. "We'll find her, son."

The others were out of their huts, seeing the commotion and crowded near my hut. I told Ash I was going to look for her.

Ash helped Miles to his feet.

I couldn't wait for Ash to coordinate the search with the others, I needed to leave now.

As if knowing what I wanted, Ash nodded his understanding, and I was off.

I knew her smell, but Claws stench was stronger. I followed the trail leading me down the mountain toward the river, only to go back up again. I stopped when I no longer smelled Ava, yet Claw's scent was overwhelming. I didn't know whether to continue on or search for her here. It was a wild goose chase, and I wanted to make Claw bleed. I ran toward his scent.

In the distance I heard the others; some had changed into their sabers and I heard their calls.

I followed Claw's scent to the forgotten cemetery, and I'd lost her scent completely. I didn't know if she was here or if Claw had done something to her along the way. Yet I hadn't seen her body.

I approached the first headstone quietly and heard Claw crying up ahead. He moaned and mumbled to himself. My chest ached as I neared. Unsure of what I'd find; if Claw had ripped Ava apart as he had done to his previous girl, and if he did, would there be anything left for me to save?

Claw sat against a headstone, his mouth bloody and partially shifted; his claws rested in his lap with flesh sticking between his sharp nails.

I swallowed the lump and closed the distance.

Claw glanced up when he heard me. "I'm sorry," he cried, sounding defeated. He'd given up.

My throat closed. My head ached. Had he destroyed her?

"What have you done?" My voice broke toward the end.

"I couldn't help myself," he whimpered. His dark brown eyes pleading with me. "She didn't want me. Nobody wanted me." He wiped his nose. "I just wanted to taste, one little bite. Help me," he whimpered desperately.

"What did you do to her?" I roared, my chest tightening and my vision blurring with rage.

"I... I couldn't stop...," he mumbled, blood dripping out his mouth and down his chin. His face shifted into his beast then back. But his claws remained sharp and deadly. He was fighting over control.

I didn't want the rage to consume me, but it did. Anger flooded my senses, and I pounced on the boy. He blocked me and pushed me off. I leaped into the air, pounding his chest with my clawed fists. He stumbled to the ground, his back hitting the headstone, and with all my strength, I hit him in the head. His head hit the gravestone, and I grabbed him, biting down as hard as I could. His blood poured down my throat, but he didn't push me away. He didn't fight me. He had given up.

Footsteps surrounded us.

Darla shrieked in the background while Ash consoled her.

I bit harder on Claw's neck, his body going limp in my jaws.

Everybody understood we couldn't allow Claw to continue. He was losing his grip on reality, twisted beyond help, and had brought enough shame to our clan.

Darla shrieked and growled. Ash asked others to help contain her.

I opened my jaws and Claw's body fell to the floor. His

claws shifted back to his hands, the gaping wound pulsed blood and his eyes clouded. I lifted my head and sniffed. Ava wasn't here.

I searched the grounds and came across three dead deers, all disemboweled, with a trail of fresh blood leading to Claw's corpse. He had been crying about the deers; confirming it was him hunting them.

Where was Ava?

Chapter Twenty

TYLER

Following Claw's scent back down toward the river, I stopped at the place where I'd lost Ava's scent.

Miles had shifted into his saber to heal the nasty wound on his head and stood beside me. He breathed in the air across his teeth and shook his head.

Ava was not here.

I glanced around, sniffed the air, and I caught the faint smell of her floral perfume. I dashed in the direction and neared the water's edge. She had somehow gotten free of Claw and swam.

Miles understood and stepped beside me.

We had never gone across the river before. The hikers on the trails would see us and everything we'd done to keep our clan hidden would be for nothing. But I had to find her. She was worth the risk.

We shifted into our human form and jumped into the water and swam across. The rapids were calm enough, and we reached the other side easily.

Scenting her while in human form wasn't ideal, but I'd

rather have the humans laugh at us because we were naked than having them scream because there were saber-tooth tigers in the mountains. It would cause confusion and the WAA would be on our asses for not disclosing ourselves to them before entering their territory.

"I smell her," Miles said beside me.

"Yeah, but he hurt her." I found dried blood she had left on a leaf as she trampled through the rough terrain and doubted she got very far with a swollen ankle. Yet she surprised me and had come this far already.

I pointed toward the path I thought she may have used, and we headed in that direction.

Chapter Twenty-One

AVA

Fighting erupted outside my hut, I yelped and jumped on the bed. A man with crazed dark eyes burst through the door, salivating.

I noticed Miles unmoving outside on the ground, and the man before me had his claws out.

"You smell better up close, pretty one," he breathed deeply, not taking his eyes off me. "Make this easy for me or hard," — he shrugged, — "either way I'm going to hurt you. Just if you come with me willingly, I won't make you bleed as much," he said menacingly, sending a nervous jolt through my body.

When that knucklehead burst through the hut door, threatening me, all I could do was obey. And I hated him for it.

"I'll not only hurt you, I'll hurt Tyler if you don't do what I ask."

In that moment I froze; sending me back to a time when my ex had spoken to me in that similar cold tone. His threats of harm and destruction. I'd come a long way since those days. And even though I didn't want to get hurt, I didn't want him to hurt Tyler.

So I did as he asked and followed. He crushed my camera beneath his enormous foot and I whimpered, he'd just killed my dreams. But I had to think of Tyler, I couldn't lose him too.

He told me his name was Claw, which suited him. His jet-black hair stuck up in all directions, he was short and skinny with big brown eyes; I didn't know where his pupils began or ended. He had a twitch on his left side, either his eyelid would flutter, or his shoulder jerked. It was unnerving. It didn't take long to figure out why his name was Claw. Whenever he twitched, his hands shifted into large claws; with one of them gripping my upper arm to keep me in place. He needed to steady his breathing before they morphed back into hands.

He frightened me; he was unstable. I wondered how they allowed him to stay in the village.

Finally, my kidnapper got distracted by a deer. His shoulder twitched, then his left eye. He made a low whining sound that made my arms pebble. When all his attention was on the deer, I used the opportunity and pushed away from him with every ounce of strength. I hobbled toward the river's edge and jumped in without thinking if this was a good idea. My thoughts crashed one on top of the other, and all I wanted to do was get away from Claw. Even though he'd threatened to hurt Tyler, I realized it was Claw who should be afraid—Tyler was much larger and powerful. I doubted Claw would see Tyler coming. I thought I needed to remove myself from Claw's plan and headed toward the river. That way, Claw couldn't threaten Tyler, because I'd be out of the equation. Leaving Tyler to sort Claw out.

My captor didn't seem to enjoy water and went after the

deer instead. I wanted to cry when I heard him attack the animals—guilt ripped through me for allowing him to do this, but I needed to get to safety. I said a silent prayer for the animals and hoped Tyler was okay. Although he was better equipped to fighting than I could ever be.

The swim across the river was a breeze, and my ankle hardly hurt. But the moment I tried to walk on the other side, I couldn't. Instead, I crawled up the mountain as fast as I could and found a safe place to rest.

Now that I was on this side, I wasn't sure Tyler would find me, but I couldn't risk crossing the river again. Not until I knew that psycho wouldn't hurt either of us.

I heard hikers a short distance away and continued in that direction. My thinking was to ask if I could borrow a phone to call the ranger for medical assistance. I noticed my captor had swiped at my back as I ran away from him; I was bleeding and needed stitches.

I finally reached the hiking trail and sat there until someone walked by.

After what felt like an hour, a couple almost had a heart attack thinking I was dead, until I reached for them. All I heard were their ear-piercing screams. Finally, after a fit of laughter, we settled down, and I asked to use their phone. They said we were a mile away from the ranger's cabin and offered to get me there. They tried their cellphones first but were out of range.

I walked between the two hikers as they helped carry me to the ranger's cabin. After every few steps I glanced over my shoulder, but no-one was following me.

An hour had passed when we finally arrived. I thanked them for their help and sank into the ranger's soft couch.

"A man has been calling for you," the ranger said as she assessed the deep gash on my shoulder. "These butterfly stitches should do the trick. You can be lucky it wasn't too deep. What did you say did this again?"

Nice try, I didn't say.

"It was a tree branch as I fell into the river. I know, I'm such a clumsy person."

"Riiight," she mumbled, but didn't push the subject.

"Did the man say who he was?"

"A Derek something—"

"He's my boss. I take photographs for his newspaper. Did he say what he wanted?"

"No, but you're welcome to use my phone." She handed me her phone and tended to my shoulder.

I knew Derek's number by heart and waited for him to pick up.

"Hello?"

"Derek, it's Ava—"

"Are you okay? I've been trying to reach you—"

"I told you where I was, remember? I went hiking."

"I remember, Ava, I'm not stupid. A man has been asking about you and I wanted to warn you."

Ice filled my veins. When I slouched my wound ached. I sat straighter and asked, "Did he give a name and what he wanted?"

"No, just that I remember you telling me about your ex when you first started working for me, and I think it's him."

This could not be happening. I didn't want to think about why he was here, or what he'd do if he found me. This was messed up.

"What did you tell him?" I finally said once I collected my thoughts.

"Nothing, I swear...." He fell silent on the other side and my stomach dropped.

"What did you tell him, Derek? I'm not angry, but I need to know if he's coming *here*."

I heard Derek swallow. "He introduced himself at golf this morning. He was talking to my parents about the pictures you took for his magazine. I didn't know who he was at first. We might have said you were hiking this weekend to get your shots for your portfolio."

I cringed and silently swore at him. "It's okay, thanks for telling me. I have to go."

"I'm sorry—"

I ended the call before he finished his sentence. Rage flooded my veins. I was careless and now he'd found me.

"Is everything okay?"

No, my ex found me. I didn't know what to do. Instead I said, "Nothing I can't handle."

When the ranger finished dressing the wound, she offered me half her sandwich and a jacket she found. She wasn't pleased when I said I had to go back on the trail. I mentioned that if anyone seemed suspicious and was looking for me; she had to call the police.

As I exited her cabin, I walked through the parking lot. It was Sunday afternoon and most of the hikers would be leaving. Some spots were already empty, with more hikers on the way to their cars. But there was one car I could never miss. The black Lexus parked beside my car.

My car was old and dirty. I ambled around another car and approached my car suspiciously. I found a card stuck to the window, held down by the wipers. I removed it from the window and read the back; *XOXO.* I knew it was him, he always ended his notes that way.

My heart raced inside my ribs and I spun around, searching the parking lot. I peered through the tinted windows of his car; there on the passenger seat was an open map book with a shell casing.

Chapter Twenty-Two

TYLER

In our naked state, Miles and I followed her bloody trail. It left me concerned for her wellbeing to have lost so much blood. But what made my chest ache was Claw biting her. We despised those who attacked humans. Were-animal bites left humans either dead or turned into the animal which bit them. I did not want Ava turning into a saber. This was not how I envisioned our relationship starting. My claiming her should not result in her turning into one of us; especially if she never wanted to in the first place.

Just thinking about what might have happened left my hands itching, and they morphed into powerful claws.

"Easy there, saber," Miles said as he stepped in front of me. "You're going to scare the hikers." He raised his hand to his ear.

I nodded and pointed to a copse nearby. Carefully, we hid between the trees and blended with the dark shadows.

Miles bumped my elbow, and I followed his line of sight. Lying in the middle of the hiking trail was Ava, giving a couple of hikers a fright when she moved while they assessed her. I smiled and my heart fluttered—she was alive but hurt.

"He scratched her," Miles confirmed in a whisper. "She will stay human."

Relief washed over me as I watched the hikers assist Ava along the trail toward the ranger's cabin.

We stealthily moved with her, ensuring her safety. I readied to pounce, naked, on top of anyone who hurt her. But it wasn't necessary.

She stayed in the ranger cabin for a while, then just when I itched to storm the cabin she emerged bandaged and her cheeks rosy. But what stopped me from approaching was the expression she wore; she was afraid. She searched the cars, removed a card from one car, and paled when she saw the black Lexus.

I wanted to go to her, but Miles held me back. There were hikers exiting the trails and heading toward their vehicles. We couldn't risk exposure.

We followed along the parking lot but kept to the rough terrain where they wouldn't see us. Ava removed something from the first car and pulled something out of the trunk. *A gun.*

Chapter Twenty-Three

AVA

I dusted glass off the back seat and popped the trunk. I needed to break the back window, I couldn't waste time going back to the village for my car keys, especially since I didn't know where it was.

I squeezed the weapon in my shaking hand. After I left Scott, I bought the gun and attended lessons. When I'd found out he was dating someone else, I kept the gun in case. Normally I avoided weapons, especially those that killed quickly, but for him I'd make an exception. I twirled a strand of my dark hair between my fingers, squeezing the gun in my other hand.

Scott had found me.

Why couldn't he have moved on?

I needed to find him first.

I couldn't allow him to find the sabers. Especially after everything they'd done to stay hidden.

I slipped the weapon inside the jacket pocket, grabbed the sandals and stepped into them. I'd lost my shoes during my swim and even though my ankle felt better, I couldn't run on it.

I glanced around the parking lot and noted a few hikers heading toward their vehicles. I closed my trunk and headed for the path.

My body ached, but I had to find Scott. I'd endured so much because of him; I would not allow him the satisfaction of hurting me again.

As I walked around a bend a short distance from where I had camped on Friday, I heard voices up ahead. I hid behind trees, carefully peering around one of them. Up ahead, Scott leaned against a tree, speaking to two female hikers. They giggled at whatever he said and I rolled my eyes. He was *not* that charming.

An uneasiness spread through me. My arms pebbled at the thought of someone helping Scott and they had found me; watching me.

I glanced over my shoulder. A surge of excitement shot through my body. It was Tyler; broad shoulders, slim hips, and butt naked. I felt my cheeks heat watching him and Miles, but I dared not glance lower.

They hurried through the brushes, closing the gap.

As Tyler neared, my heart fluttered inside my chest and I approached—meeting him halfway.

"How did you find me?" I whispered, glancing over my shoulder but no-one could see us from our position.

"Are you okay?"

"Yes."

"We need to leave, Ava. Miles and I can't stay out here like this."

"Okay, but we have a bigger problem."

Tyler arched an eyebrow.

"Remember when I told you about my ex, and that he wasn't a problem."

"Yeah," he said hesitantly.

"He's a problem now and he's here."

Tyler peered over my head. "Is that him?"

I nodded.

"Is that why you have the gun?"

"How did you know?"

"We saw you. We need to go this way." He pointed to the side. "There's no way he can find our village."

"What if he finds it?"

"There's no way he can find it, Ava. I promise."

I exhaled a frustrated breath and followed closely behind Tyler with Miles behind me. It felt strange walking between two naked men. But I wasn't thinking about that as we traversed away from the path and away from Scott.

I wondered how Scott had found me. I hadn't had my picture in any of the articles I'd given Derek, nor was I listed anywhere. I used my mother's maiden name for the rental apartment and I paid everything in cash. I no longer used credit cards or anything that he could use to trace me. I'd stopped using contract phones, unless... Scott had managed to get my number from Derek.

The muscles between my shoulder blades tightened, and I felt on edge.

By the time we reached their village, the sun had started to set. We had evaded Scott, yet I kept glancing over my shoulder.

I followed Tyler to his hut, passed a crying woman while others hummed a tune I'd never heard before. I smelled incense burning and in the centre something wrapped in white material. I touched Tyler's back as he stepped toward his hut.

"What happened?"

"I killed the man who took you," he said nonchalantly, and entered the hut. "He was also killing the deer in the area. We can't afford to attract the authorities. If any of them found out someone was hunting the wild animals, they'd descend upon us without thinking. We couldn't allow that. He was putting our lives in danger," he added gravely.

I felt bad, but Claw was dangerous. He could've hurt me, and he threatened Tyler.

"We will do a proper send off for his mother." Tyler jerked his chin toward the crying woman. "Hopefully things will settle down."

Tyler stopped near the doorjamb, pulled me closer and cupped my face. "I should've done this when I found you on the trail."

His lips touched mine, and I didn't hold back. I opened my mouth to his, our tongues tangling. An explosion of nerve endings rocked my body as his naked body twitched against mine.

I quivered as his hands trailed down my waist, over my ass and I forgot about our surroundings. I felt like I was the only person in his world and he was the only one in mine. Just the two of us, together; I heard no sounds, apart from my beating heart, in tune with his. I only felt the heat from his body as it surrounded me, comforting me. And I kissed him with my heart, and my soul.

When he ended the kiss, my eyes flitted open, but his

were still closed. When he finally opened them, they glowed yellow, and a smile spread across his face.

He licked his lips. "That was divine." He closed the gap for a peck on my cheek and I just stared at him.

My body felt like jelly. After a moment had passed, I remembered where I was and what we were doing. The sting of Scott being nearby left me cold and slightly bitter. *Why did he have to come now?*

I glanced down, the door was on the floor, completely ripped out of its hinges. I stepped over it and entered the hut.

"I'll fix it," he said and pulled on jeans.

Miles walked past and entered the hut next to ours.

My cellphone lit up. There were a dozen messages from Derek and double the amount of missed phone calls. That man was impossible. I read the messages and instead of texting him back; I phoned him. When he answered, he wanted to know if I was safe and whether Scott had found me. I put his mind at ease saying I'd be leaving for the police station soon but before I ended the call I asked if Scott had ever held his phone. Derek said their phones were together on the table, but he did stand up to fetch something, leaving his phone on the table.

While I was busy speaking to Derek, Tyler had put the door back, but it hung skew.

When I ended the call I laughed, and it put Tyler at ease because he laughed too.

When my phone lit up again, I frowned.

"What's going on?"

"I think Scott has my number."

The screen lit up followed by a chime, as if someone had a 'Find my phone' app installed and was actively seeking my phone.

I glanced wide eyed at Tyler who understood what it meant.

"If he's coming here we need to prepare. We need to ensure he doesn't find my village," he said and stormed out of the hut.

Tyler approached a man, informing him of the situation.

I felt guilty for what was happening. If I'd known Scott was anywhere near Derek, trying to get to me, I wouldn't have hiked the weekend. I would've put as much distance between us as possible. I also didn't like the fact that I'd brought Scott here and didn't want anyone getting hurt because of me.

I kicked off my sandals and pulled on my second pair of hiking boots, pocketing my pistol and knife. Staying here like bait wasn't an option, nor waiting for Scott to enter Tyler's village and shoot one of them. I'd rather lead Scott away and try to take care of this myself.

Grabbing my phone, I exited the hut and walked around and away from everyone. The phone continued making that sound; I silenced it but kept it in my hand. I tried to reverse engineer the app, but it blocked me—I didn't know how close Scott was.

My phone vibrated. I stopped to see what was going on, but the screen died. Twigs snapped behind me. I spun around and there he stood.

"Ava, my sweet Ava. Do you know how long I've tried to find you."

"Get away from me, Scott. It's been more than a year."

"No, you ran away—"

"Because you hit me."

"I'm sorry, babe. I truly am. Please, can we try one more time?"

I shook my head, pulling out my weapon and pointing it at him. He raised his hands.

"Tsk, tsk. I thought you hated guns."

"You've made it necessary."

Scott stepped closer. I stepped back. He lunged at me, hitting the gun out of my hands. His shoulder collided with my chest, knocking the wind out of me. We fell to the ground with him on top. He grabbed my head, slamming it to the ground. My vision tunneled and darkness swallowed me.

Chapter Twenty-Four

AVA

I awoke upside down. My blood rushing to my head, giving me a splitting headache. I watched Scott's sneakers as he carried me. My head pounded louder with each painful step he took. I tried to move my arms, but they felt heavy and cold. He'd tied my arms behind my back, straining my shoulders while my stomach ached colliding with his shoulder with each step.

"Please untie me," I breathed. "I can't…" I sucked in air. "Please…" I tried tightening my stomach muscles but I couldn't maintain that position for long. "I won't run away."

Scott stopped, tugged on my body and the ground moved. Then the sky moved above me as he set me on my feet.

Feeling rushed back into my arms and my feet tingled.

"Good, now that you're awake you can walk yourself." He pulled on my upper arm, forcing me to walk beside him.

"Why are you doing this? You can have any girl you want…" What I really wanted to say was no girl sane enough would stick with him. He was too possessive and saw women as toys for his enjoyment and whenever he pleased.

"Yeah, and I had a lot of them. But," — he shrugged, — "you got away."

I rolled my eyes and stopped, giving him my meanest look. "I really liked you at first, Scott. But then you tried to own me. If you kidnap me now, understand I'll do everything in my power to get away from you. Please, just untie me and go away. I promise not to call the cops."

He slowly shook his head. His menacing expression left my body cold. His haunted stare pierced straight through my face.

"I can't do that. You need to be punished for what you've put me through. I waited an entire year for this; the right moment."

I didn't want to wait any longer. I kicked his shin and ran in the opposite direction, running as fast as I could manage with my aching ankle. It was difficult because my hands were behind my back. But I managed as I dashed off the path, down the mountain, and just when I thought I got away, a weight landed on top of me. I hit the ground hard. My head smashed into the dirt, and I tasted the earth. The last thing I thought was he was going to kill me.

Chapter Twenty-Five

TYLER

"Where is she?" I yelled for all to hear. The hut was empty and her hiking boots were gone. She went after him. *Alone.* My beast rippled under my skin, pleading for release. *Soon!*

She didn't want her ex coming to my village. I loved how she thought of my people, but she was stubborn; we could've done this together.

"Miles," I called him over and Blaze followed.

"Help me," I growled and told them the rest of the story. "I know none of this is her fault, and it's not our fight. But we need to help her. He's put her in the hospital before, I don't want her hurt."

My saber growled. He didn't like that she was with the man who had hurt her.

We needed to bring her back. Now!

The three of us shifted into our beasts and followed her scent. We sprinted down the mountain and picked up her scent. We followed the trail and found some blood—*her blood.* My beast snarled at the discovery. He hurt our woman. We needed to stay focused and continued following her scent until we reached the hiking path.

Darkness surrounded us. The smell of the earth and damp leaves around us as the world sped past us. Her scent was stronger the farther we ran on the hiking trail. I didn't care if there were hikers; I had to find Ava before Scott hurt her.

Up ahead was the parking lot and the cars. The doors of the black Lexus stood open. A man bundled something into the backseat, slamming the door closed.

I growled. The man glanced up, frozen to the spot, then fumbled for something behind his back. He turned around, aiming his weapon at us.

"No!" yelled Ava from the backseat. She squeezed her body between the two seats as she stared at me, shaking her head.

It was then I realized she saw my true form, my saber. She'd glimpsed me in the dim light of the oil lamp, but now she saw the real me under the bright street light.

Would she accept this, accept me? She mouthed the words *'you're beautiful,'* giving me the boost to get rid of this guy.

A deep guttural sound came from the back of our throats, warning him.

"What the?" Scott said, his hand shaking. He fired his gun.

It missed Blaze, who snapped his jaws. I lunged at Scott. We tussled. He tried to push me off but I was too big. He managed to move his hand and I felt the steel against me. Shots rang off. I opened my jaw and went for his jugular. I wanted him dead. When another round of shots hit my body, I let go of his neck, staggered to the other side of the car, and collapsed.

Miles jumped over me, landing on Scott.

Chapter Twenty-Six

AVA

After my second hospital admission, I'd learned my shoulder could pop out of the socket easily with barely any pain. I needed to get free of Scott because the moment he climbed into the car and started it, I'd be dead.

I twisted my arms, my shoulder popped, my arm went limp, and I slipped my arms under my legs and over to have them in front of me again. I slammed my shoulder into the front seat; popping it back into place. I clenched my jaw until the pain subsided. I hadn't done it in a while and it was a shock to my system. My vision tunneled from the sudden burst of pain while my head throbbed and continued to bleed. I was not having a great day.

I watched the three sabers approach while Scott aimed the gun at Tyler. I recognized Tyler's furry body, but it was the look in his eyes; glowing yellow and filled with concern—*for me*. But, he seemed worried about something… I didn't know why? He shuffled his paws and dropped his head. I caught the despondent line on his shoulders. A flurry of emotions swirled around me; he was concerned for my safety but also worried about what I thought of him in his saber form.

His yellow eyes stayed on mine and I smiled mouthing the words, *'you're beautiful,'* which made him raise his head and turn his dark gaze on Scott once more.

Shots went off. I focused my attention on Scott and Tyler on the ground. They scuffled. Tyler was huge compared to him but Scott fought dirty. When more shots rang, I freaked, twisted my hands in opposite directions until the cable ties snapped apart.

I opened the backdoor when Tyler scrambled to the front of my car and another saber jumped onto Scott.

My heart stopped as my world slowed. Tyler fell to the ground, bleeding. My throat closed, fearing the worst.

Shots sounded again. I focused on the saber clawing Scott's hand, ripping it from his arm and it went flying to the other side with the gun landing nearby. Scott swore and cried out as he clutched his bloody stump to his chest with his good hand around his neck—but the neck wound was superficial.

The saber stalking Scott looked ready to pounce and rip his head off.

My eyes flitted to Tyler, who lay motionless on the ground. My chest squeezed as I struggled for air; tears streaming down my face.

Scott bumped into my legs as he shuffled away from the other saber, and glanced up at me.

"What the fuck, Ava?" he mumbled, but his eyes were pleading for me to help him.

I shook my head, stared at the saber, and nodded.

Scott didn't deserve my comfort. He deserved much worse. But I was not like him and never would be. I could never allow anyone to be hurt on purpose, no matter what they did to me.

"If you want to live, I'd suggest you climb into your Lexus and seek immediate treatment. And if you don't leave me alone, my new friends will tear you a new one."

Scott climbed to his feet, and pushed his bloody stump into my chest as he swayed. I pushed him against his car while I opened his door for him.

The saber remained in the same spot while Scott sat behind the wheel and fumbled with his keys. I grabbed them out of his good hand and pressed the start button, his car roared to life.

Before closing his door, I grabbed a shirt and ripped it up to make a tourniquet, then continued strapping his stump and his neck so he wouldn't bleed to death.

A saber stood and morphed into his human form; a large, well-built and very naked man with ice-blue eyes. He stared at Scott, and I was sure he could kill with that look. He picked up Scott's severed hand and threw it at me; I handed it to Scott. Then the other saber pointed and said coldly. "If you ever come for her again, you will die."

I slammed the door as Scott put his car in reverse and backed up.

The other saber and Miles darted for Tyler who was now in his human form and struggling to breathe.

"He took two shots to the chest. Help me carry him," Miles said.

"We must go to hospital."

"No," the other man said. "We have a healer within our community. He will know what to do." He glanced nervously at Miles and they picked up Tyler.

Chapter Twenty-Seven

AVA

With every agonizing step, Tyler winced. The walk back was long and difficult even though the other two helped carry him. But because Tyler was so much larger than them, they struggled.

By the time we arrived at the village he was still bleeding. Relief washed over me when others ran up to us, helping the other two carry him.

I received stares that left me chilled, and I felt horribly guilty. If I could trade places with him, I would. This was my fault and I wished there was something I could do to make it better.

"Bring him here," an old man said. He was ancient, with leathery skin, and one good eye. He tied his silver hair in a low ponytail, wore a loincloth, and used a stick to aid him as he walked. "Come," he rambled and entered a hut on the far side of the village.

I followed Miles into the hut when the other man, I now knew as Blaze, shoved his fingers into my chest and pushed me outside.

"You are not part of my people. If it wasn't for you, this wouldn't have happened." He lowered his hand but continued to give me his death stare.

I swallowed the large lump in my throat but stood my ground. "I know. Everything is my fault and I'm terribly sorry. If I could take it back, I would. If there's anything I can do to help, I want to." My voice croaked toward the end as I swallowed my tears.

"You're not welcome here," Blaze said in a bitter tone that left me shivering.

Miles ran out to comfort me. "Ignore Blaze, he's just upset. Allow Windtalker to assess the damage to Tyler first. Wait over there," — he pointed at a patch of grass, — "and I'll fetch you."

I nodded, sat down and dusted tears from my face, but they didn't stop flowing.

My heart tugged and ached for Tyler, and I wished I could exchange places with him.

I succumbed to exhaustion, but the moment someone exited the hut I shot up as if electrocuted by an invisible cord.

The old man crouched near me. "My dear, the bullet stopped too close to his heart and I can't get it. You need to brace yourself that there's the possibility he may not make it."

I blinked back the tears. "Is there anything we can do?"

"There is a way—"

"Anything, if you need me to do something, please tell me," I said with some excitement.

He smiled sincerely and nodded once. "What do you know about the shifter bonding?"

I frowned at him and shrugged. I didn't know much. I'd learned a few things at school but they'd said it was different for each were-animal.

He stood and proffered his hand. "Walk with me."

Windtalker curled his bony fingers around my elbow and we ambled around the village while he explained what he meant by shifter bonding. We received stares, well I received stares, some scowled, and one even snarled at me displaying their elongated teeth. I shuffled closer to Windtalker as he described the ceremony.

When a shifter found his or her true mate and they bonded, it was for life. It was the equivalent of finding your true love—*one you'd stay with forever*. He spoke of how he had felt *something* the last couple of days where he suspected Tyler had laid claim to me but hadn't closed the bonding ritual. He surmised Tyler wanted to make sure I was the right one for him. And possibly if it was something I wanted. Windtalker didn't know how I felt about Tyler. But, as stubborn as Tyler was, Windtalker knew I was the right one for him.

It explained why my body reacted to Tyler in that way and how I felt at home in his embrace. I wanted to be near him. Always. But being stubborn myself, I thought nothing of it. It felt like an intense crush, which I denied.

As Windtalker spoke, I wasn't sure whether being bound to someone for the rest of my life was something I wanted. We barely knew each other. *Was he really the one?*

Then flashes of Tyler lying unconscious as Blaze and Miles had carried him tugged at the deepest part of my heart. He didn't think twice to help me, to save me. He had searched when Claw had taken me and had even killed Claw. He had cared for me in a way no man had ever. And as much as I tried to deny it, I was falling for him and knew it to be true. I glanced around, taking in the magnificent sight before me. It was then I knew what I wanted. I saw myself living here with Tyler and his clan.

And if there was a way I could help Tyler, I wanted to do it.

I swallowed the lump and asked the question. "What do you need me to do?"

Windtalker had said there was a way we could speed up Tyler's healing. He was too weak for us to bond in this world, but there was another way to bond in the spirit realm. If it worked, and we bonded, Tyler could use the power from within the clan and the earth at our feet to heal his wounds.

They had managed to remove the second bullet but left the bullet near his heart for fear of further damage. He'd already lost too much blood and was too weak to shift into his saber, therefore unable to heal himself. His heart had failed to beat steadily, instead it was slowing down, weakening him some more. They'd done what they could, now it was up to Tyler to heal himself.

I offered to call Ruth, but Windtalker shook his head. A wildlife veterinarian wouldn't know how to help Tyler and there wasn't enough time to get him to a hospital that catered to were-animal injuries. Tyler was dying.

Windtalker offered me a vial of a liquid called Naimoi, similar to Ayahuasca. It would enlighten me and send me to a place where I could find Tyler, bond with him, and hopefully he'd use the clan's power to heal. It was something shifters took to speak with those long gone; and never meant for humans and the threat of me staying there, or dying, was real.

If this was Tyler's only hope, I'd do it. Now that I had the time to think about it—and what I wanted—I didn't want to live without him. I couldn't see myself living another day without him and would do all I could to help, even if it meant risking my life.

Everybody had left Tyler and me alone. I carefully lay beside him, kissed his cheek and a chill went through me; he was in his human form, cold, pale, and his lips were turning blue. His chest barely rose and fell. Since he was unable to heal himself, blood pooled beneath him, and they covered the wound on his chest with medicinal leaves.

He was on the brink of death; doing this for him was my only chance to help him.

I said a silent prayer for guidance and strength. Tears streaked my face. My heart ached seeing him so still, so hurt.

I raised the vial to my mouth and drank it down. The bitter taste left me nauseated and my stomach ached. Fire coursed through my veins, burning me. My vision blurred, and I nestled against Tyler's side, holding him tightly against me. If this was my last breath then I wanted it to be by his side, and I breathed in his scent.

In that moment, I forgot about my pictures and portfolio. I forgot about my TV dinners for one and how my life used to be. I only thought of Tyler, how he made me feel and how I loved being around him.

My body heated from the Naimoi, then I drifted to sleep.

Chapter Twenty-Eight

TYLER

I ran through the woods; my saber pushing to go faster and farther. The trees blurred past me as I headed toward the water, reflecting the bright light. Others stood around, waiting for me. I glimpsed my mother in the distance and I ran toward her. I saw my ancestors, and I raced to meet them once more. I felt content. I was at home with my people; those who had passed long before me.

But…

This didn't feel right. I wasn't ready to go to them. Not yet. I stopped, shaking my head. There was something I was forgetting. There was something important I needed to do. I couldn't remember what had brought me here. Did I fight Claw? Did I fight Ash? Why was I…

I glanced over my shoulder at the forest behind me and my heart tugged and skipped a beat. I smelled her scent.

Ava.

No, I didn't want to go toward the light—not yet. I needed to find Ava. I needed to see her one last time.

I felt her presence—*here*—and I needed to find her.

With every part of my being, I hoped she wasn't dead.

I turned around, ignoring the calls to go to my mother, to go to my ancestors. Instead, I followed her scent. I blurred past trees and bushes until I found her sitting on a fallen log. She seemed peaceful and serene. She sat with her hands between her legs, her eyes were closed and a smile tugged on her lips. The fine slope of her nose, her thin, kiss-able lips, and her beauty pulled me closer.

She opened her honey-colored eyes, and smiled sweetly.

"You came." She stood and ran to me. She clung to my furry body and scratched my soft fur.

I rubbed my large head against hers, careful not to cut her with my sizable canines.

"How are you here?" I asked nervously, afraid of what the answer would be.

She told me about the injury I'd suffered while trying to get her away from her ex, the bullet striking close to my heart and my body lying in Windtalker's hut.

"Windtalker gave me a vial of something gross to drink. He said it was the only way to help you. We needed to bond."

The bonding ritual—*of course*. We hardly used this method amongst our kind, but it had worked before. But she was only human and had risked her life to be here; coming to my aid. My heart swelled with love for this woman and all I wanted to do was embrace her. To pull her into my arms and never let go. To kiss all over her body and make her *mine*.

I glanced down at my saber form and knew I needed to change. It felt strange needing to be human in our spirit world, but I had to do it for her. The bonding couldn't work otherwise.

Slowly I stood tall, my transition back into my human

form felt odd; tendons pulled, bones snapped and reformed. In moments I stood with my arms around her naked body. She clung to me, her legs over mine, her arms around my neck, afraid to let me go. I pulled her closer and kissed her with my heart and my soul. My life bound to hers, *forever*.

A thought gnawed on me then, I'd never spoken to her about the bonding ceremony and didn't know if it was something she even wanted. She had shown she wanted to spend time with me, but mentioned nothing about a lifelong bonding.

"Now that you know what it means, is this what you really want?"

She lifted her head away from my shoulder and smiled. "I've wanted nothing more in my life. I've barely known you for a week, but it feels as though my soul has known you a lifetime. I don't know how, or why, but the more I thought about it, the more I realized it's true. I want to spend the rest of my life with you." She pressed her soft lips against mine and I crushed her against me.

She was so soft in my arms, leaving me hard against her delicate flesh.

"So is that a yes?" I asked in between kisses.

She playfully smacked my shoulder and broke the kiss. Her eyes twinkled with humor. "Of course. I do."

I gently crushed her to the soft grass and positioned myself between her legs. Warmth spread through me and into her as I nudged the tip of my cock against her slick opening. She spread her legs wider for me and her warm hands reached for my ass, pulling me toward her. I slipped inside her, so soft, so warm, so mine. The scent of her arousal filled my nostrils, going straight to my heart.

I felt how she wanted me as much as I wanted her. We

may have only known each other for a short time, but our connection was strong. We shared that spark I craved.

I feathered kisses along her neck and opened myself to her. It wasn't just desire, and it was more than love. It was the need to offer myself to her, allowing her into my soul and offering her everything I had.

She met each long stroke with her own as she too offered herself to me; her warmth traveled through my body and struck my heart—melding us together.

Ava had given so much of herself and risked her life by being here only made me love her more.

Our bodies became one; our hearts joined, and our souls entwined.

How a chance encounter had brought us together, with near death sealing our fate.

A forbidden love with a human, yet it was a human who saved me. I would spend my days making her happy, and I'd do so gladly.

Chapter Twenty-Nine

AVA

I felt every delicious inch of him slide into me, filling me, making me his. I felt his desire swirl around me, his pleasure delighting me, but it was the warmth of his love that bound me to him.

Tyler offered me his soul, and his heart; the least I could do was give him the same.

I met each of his thrusts time and time again, clenching my body around his hard shaft. With each stroke, I felt a part of my soul shatter, coming together and made whole with his. I loved the man above me with every inch of my being, and I kissed his soft lips. He bruised my lips with his love and I whimpered in pleasure.

It was in that moment our bodies joined and we became one; carnal creatures in heat, tangling and writhing in a brutal mating dance.

He took us over the edge as skin slapped skin and we came together; I reveled in the sensation as his passionate waves knocked me over and he grunted as he poured his heat inside me.

My hands greedily roamed over his hot, sweaty skin for a last embrace before he left me, collapsing beside me.

Chapter Thirty

TYLER

The surrounding air shimmered with the powerful bond, strengthening us.

I felt the power swirl around me, coursing through me, giving me strength and vitality.

I felt stronger, rejuvenated, whole.

I pulled more of the power within me. The bullet moved; I winced as it slowly exited away from my heart and out of my body. My wounds knitted together. And my heart pumped stronger.

This was the power of my clan. Together much was possible. And I would ensure we had a fruitful future.

I reached for my woman, pulling her closer, and we floated away.

Chapter Thirty-One

TYLER

We woke in each other's arms, in Windtalker's hut. I pulled Ava toward me, never wanting to let her go. I caressed her waist, the calluses on my fingers hard against her soft skin.

"Wow, I didn't think... but... just wow," she rambled, licking her dry lips and reached for my face.

I leaned down and crushed myself against her. "Thank you," I said and kissed her. When I pulled away her eyes sparkled with unshed tears.

"I'm sorry for everything. I thought—"

"Shh," — I placed my index finger over her lips,— "I know it wasn't your fault. And I'm sorry I scared you. I'll try not to let it happen again," I whispered. She smiled sadly. There was a question burning on my lips, and I had to know. "Do you regret it?"

"Oh never," she said, pulling me toward her again. "I would do it again. I'm happy to be yours."

The clan were grateful to Ava for saving my life, although one or two didn't appreciate her bringing the trouble to our clan. But, none of it would've happened if I hadn't brought her to our village in the first place. And then again I'm glad I did, otherwise I wouldn't have had her by my side, and she would most likely have ended up dead when her ex showed up. I thought it worked out perfectly.

After greeting and introducing her to everyone, we met with Ash. He sat outside his hut with Darla who sat near her son's body. They had to postpone Claw's burial till today because they waited for me—for us—to recover.

Darla didn't look our way but I felt her hatred radiating off her in waves. I ignored her.

"Ava," Ash said, pulling her into an embrace.

I stood with a mouth full of teeth, I was not expecting that kind of greeting from him. His eyes glistened when he turned to me, bringing me into an embrace. I allowed him his comfort and tapped his shoulder to let him know he could let me go.

"You saved my boy."

"Well, it was my fault, so,"— she shrugged, — "I couldn't leave him there," she grinned.

"Ugh," Darla moaned and spat near our feet. "You make me sick, you know. She isn't even one of us. She's a weak human."

"Darla!" Ash yelled, that one word a silent warning.

"Don't *Darla* me, Ash. And when she has your pups," — she pointed a finger at me, — "she's going to die. Just like your weak mother."

"Darla!" Ash stormed her, yanking her to her feet. "This is your last warning."

"You know," — she shoved Ash away, — "I've always wanted to tell you what really happened that day. Your mom was alive," she said, glowering at me. "I helped clean her, dressed her wounds. But the moment she carried on about your father and how the three of you were going to live together like one big happy family, I couldn't take it anymore. I've always loved your dad. And no matter what I did he always chose her. He only wanted her. But she was so weak, she couldn't even clean herself. And you know what I did—"

"Don't say it," Ash said, his voice breaking. He stepped away from her and threw something into the fire.

Other clan members joined behind us, wanting to hear Darla's confession.

"And I smothered her. There, I said it. It's out." She squeezed her eyes shut. "Just kill me now."

I fisted my hands, ready to give her her wish when Ava caught my arm. I stared into those honey-colored eyes, she shook her head and mouthed, 'Don't'. I pulled her into the curve of my shaking body. Rage filled me, gnashing my teeth as I thought of ways to hurt Darla. She'd killed my mother and had stolen those precious years from me. I wanted her to suffer. I wanted her dead.

Blaze and Miles approached Darla, each taking an arm.

"What do you want to do with her?" Miles asked Ash.

Ash's shoulders sagged and he wiped away tears. "She doesn't deserve the easy way out. She needs to suffer for the rest of her life. If she wants to die she can do so by her own hand. But I refuse to be the one offering her death." Ash approached Darla, stared down at her and added. "Grab your stuff and leave. I don't want you near our people ever again. If you return, I will ensure you receive only pain." He went back to the fire and removed the branding iron from the flames.

"No, Ash, please. I'd rather you kill me."

Ash shook his head. "Keep her still."

Blaze and Miles did as Ash asked and he pressed the branding iron with the words, *impius*, onto her chest, a symbol marking a saber who couldn't be trusted, was wicked, disloyal, and sinful.

Darla's shrill cries echoed around us. Her tears staining her cheeks.

"And take your son with you," Ash said, his cold tone made my arms pebble. He turned his back on her and entered his hut.

Everybody turned their back on Darla and went to their respective huts.

I took Ava by the hand, taking her to her new home.

Ava had quit her job and moved her things into my small hut. She would fill her days taking pictures of wildlife and finish her portfolio.

Now that Ash had accepted her, a human, into our clan we were no longer bound to secrecy. I attended a meeting with Ash at the WAA, where they welcomed us and agreed to us remaining in this part of the forest. But, we had to behave. If any one of us stepped out of line they'd force us out.

Ash had agreed to step down now that I had bonded, and would live the rest of his life fishing.

I made Blaze my second in command and head of security, while Miles was content being my third.

Now that our presence was known within Sterling Meadow, the rest of the clan were free to go into town without having to mask their true selves.

I traced my hand down the sides of Ava's curvy body. They were my curves now. I smirked at the thought.

She pressed her ass against my cock and wiggled. I slapped her right ass cheek, positioned myself behind her, gripped her hips and slammed my body inside. Before I'd been holding back, I was gentle. But now I knew what her body could handle, and I was no longer hurt—or afraid I'd hurt her. I crashed into her over and over with sweet delectable thrusts inside her heated sheath, she coated me in her slick juices and we floated into bliss.

Her hands pressed against the wall as I brought us over. She squeezed around my cock and I released my seed within. I let go of her hips and trailed my hands up to her breasts and eased my strokes, slowly bringing us back to earth.

She fisted the walls as she came again with one final thrust.

"Oh gods," she mumbled as she caught her breath. "I love them quick and dirty sometimes."

I pulled out and she turned around slowly.

"I love you." She clutched my shoulders and I kissed her with my everything.

"I love you, too."

Next in the Shifter Days, Vampire
Nights, & Demons in between Series

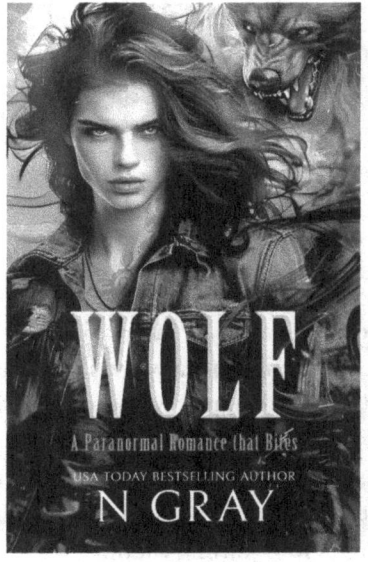

www.vinci-books.com/wolf

A Dangerous Dance of Fur and Fury.

I despise shifters with every fibre of my being. Except for Jason's
divine coffee—and those magnetic eyes behind the counter. When
violence erupts in his café, my sworn enemy becomes my shield.
Now I'm caught between old hatred and new hunger that refuses
to be denied.

Turn the page for a free preview…

Wolf: Chapter One

CLAIRE

Today was going to be a great day—I could feel it. Everything was going to go my way. I'd woken on the right side of the bed. My makeup was just right, and my hair was behaving. I was ready to start my Friday with a spring in my step. My bosses had started a new case and said I could join them if I wanted to. But I'd first see how much admin still needed finishing before joining them.

My jeans slipped over my hips and butt without effort or needing to suck in my stomach; the latest exercise routine I'd started was working. I'd lost some weight, although I still had a few pounds to go. I'd gained some muscle and hadn't felt better in years. I never thought my late thirties were going to be this hard, and was dreading my forties, even though it was only three years away.

The only thing that could upset me today was the awfully long queue outside my favorite coffee shop. I grumbled to myself when I stood behind a man speaking to someone on his phone, writing down the list of coffee orders. This was going to take forever.

Unfortunately, I was as mundane as humans came and couldn't freeze the line, so I could cut in front. I'd have to wait like the rest of the sheeple for my delicious cappuccino.

There were other coffee shops in Sterling Meadow, but this one I *loved*. Their coffees were smooth, rich, and mouth-watering. I only had one tiny addiction—coffee. I wasn't a connoisseur, per se, but I liked what I liked. And this coffee was the absolute best; *magnifique*, as the French would say.

The line moved, and I was finally inside the shop. Peering around the shoulders of the man in front of me, I glimpsed at the counter. I moaned inwardly and hoped the owner didn't see me. Not that I didn't like Jason; he was gorgeous to look at, but... there was always a *but*. He was a wolf. An alpha were-wolf part of Shawn's pack. And he owned the best freaking coffee in town. What alpha wolf, in his right mind, did that? A man like him should be out doing wolf stuff, not mess with my coffee, or bake the best muffins. Yet, it was his coffee I craved and bought daily.

"Claire!" boomed his voice from behind the counter. "Your order is ready."

If this was any other coffee shop, I'd gladly smile and head over to the front, passing all the waiting suckers. But this was Jason's coffee shop, and I'd hoped he wasn't in today. The moon was full last night, and his kind usually hunted all night and slept all day. But he wasn't sleeping. No, not this man. He had to be in his shop, staring right at me.

I didn't like him much. But I wanted my coffee more. I sucked up my ego, avoided eye contact with the other patrons as I passed them, and headed for the counter.

I felt Jason's dark gaze rake over my body, and I wanted to squirm. When I glanced up, his smiling blue eyes pene-trated mine, and I touched my clothing instinctively—I still had my clothing on and nobody else was watching me. It was only Jason's intense stare, making me feel this way.

Jason wasn't drop-dead-drool-all-over-yourself kind of gorgeous; he was ruggedly handsome. He had a slightly crooked nose, a scar on his chin which was hidden beneath his short brown beard, and one ear was slightly pointy at the top. I may have been staring at him for longer than necessary, but then again, he was staring back.

And he was a were-wolf.

I couldn't say for sure when I started hating were-wolves. I just did. They smelled like the earth, powerfully built, and most of them exuded dominant sex pheromones that tested my ovaries.

My core spasmed, and I shoved that feeling down and glowered at Jason when he approached the counter with a delectable smile.

"I didn't order yet," I said softly so only his super ears heard.

"After all these months you've been coming into my coffee shop, you'd think I wouldn't know your order by now?" he asked rhetorically, pushing the takeaway cup and bag filled with two warm chocolate muffins that oozed chocolate bits my way. His large, powerful hands lingered on my items. The muscles on his tanned forearms bunched. I wondered if he was testing me and whether I'd touch his hands when I took my order from him.

My mouth watered. I wanted. Give me. Now! My anger dissolved on my tongue, and I fished for the money.

I flinched when an enormous hand touched mine. My gaze travelled up his muscular forearm until I reached his pleasantly smiling face.

"My treat," he said with a gruff, masculine voice.

"I don't want to owe you anything," I said and slapped

money on the counter. "Keep the change." I grabbed my goodies and hurried out the door before he stopped me.

There was something wrong with that man. I didn't know why Jason did that to me, but he did, and I hated it. I hated him. But after one sip of his coffee, I practically melted onto the sidewalk. It was orgasmic. And the chocolate muffin. Oh my gods, better than sex.

My thoughts drifted to a dark bedroom with a naked Jason, and I shook the vision away with a shudder. That would never happen. Besides, someone like him probably dated all the women in town, and I didn't want to be just another notch on his very long and very thick belt. Oh, gods... I didn't even want to go there.

Besides, I had a boyfriend. Which reminded me. I pulled out my cellphone and sent Erik a text message about our date tonight. It was our six-month anniversary, and I had a sneaky suspicion he was about to ask me to move in with him. I was so excited. Things were finally going well for me. Erik still gave me butterflies in my stomach when we touched. That had to mean something.

Erik was one of those silent, sensitive types, while I was slightly on the loud and wild side compared to him. And ever since I'd met him, I'd calmed down a little, because I wanted things to work out between us. Erik was a late bloomer, and I was the first person he'd ever slept with. I never made him feel embarrassed about that fact, ever. He was seven years my junior, but he was mature for his age.

I enjoyed the rest of my muffin, threw the empty liner in the trash can and pocketed the second muffin. I climbed the three steps and entered the building where I worked. Our office was on the fifth floor, but I hardly saw my bosses; Blaire and Ralph. Ulysses Assassins was a monster contract killer agency that became a legal entity when they started working with the police. I was a recent addition to the team because they were so busy, they needed someone to do their administration, legal paperwork, and even balance the books. Since I was a brainiac, although I never finished college, I taught myself how to do everything and I did it well. Blaire had even given me a bonus last month because I'd caught up with all their admin.

I reached my floor and came across Josh, the little five-year-old brat who belonged to the lawyer across the hallway. He was a busy-body but in hindsight a very sweet kid.

"What you got there?" he asked inquisitively, his big brown eyes staring at my bulging pocket.

"It's a surprise. Do you want to see it?"

He nodded so vigorously I thought his head was about to fly off.

"I got you a special muffin again today. Do you want it?" Yesterday I brought him a bran muffin, and it surprised me that Jason had packed two chocolate muffins today without me asking. I smiled at the thought, then frowned at his audacity. I should've appreciated it, but he was a were-animal, a were-wolf, and I hated them all.

Josh's smile split his face in two, and he held out his hands. The office door where his mom worked opened, and she stood in the doorjamb, her slender figure silhouetted by the light behind her.

"Josh! I hope you aren't pestering Claire, again?"

"It's fine, Lucy. Can I give him a muffin?"

"Thanks, Claire. You can," Lucy said, then her voice changed to that commanding tone that made me want to do everything she asked. "Then you come back here, Josh. You know I don't like it when you wander around."

"Thank you, Miss Claire." Josh grabbed the muffin out of my hands and ran to his mother.

I unlocked and entered my office, set my half-empty cup on my desk, switched on my laptop, and sat behind my desk to start working.

Blaire had asked whether I wanted to work from home. Although I loved my home, my apartment was too small to live and work in the same space. I'd go insane, and she'd have to visit me at that special ward, providing care for those in dire need.

My inbox pinged with all the new emails, and I started my workday.

Wolf: Chapter Two

CLAIRE

I finished work around five. On my way home, I had to pass Jason's coffee shop, which was aptly named '*Alpha Coffee*'. I snorted at the irony. The doors were already closed, and the lights were off. From what I knew, Jason kept it open till about three in the afternoon. What he did to fill the rest of his time, I didn't know. He was probably at his pack's club-house, or whatever they called it.

When I arrived home, I got ready for my date with Erik.

Erik had texted letting me know he was coming directly to the restaurant after work and asked that I meet him there.

I dressed in my stylish jeans, and wore a pretty blouse with a jacket over it. I managed to put on some makeup, making me feel ready to tackle the world.

At seven o'clock I entered our favorite Italian place and found our regular table at the back which Erik had reserved for our date. I ordered a couple of whiskeys for us and perused the menu while I waited for him.

After thirty minutes and two whiskeys later, Erik finally arrived, looking a bit disheveled.

"What happened to you?" I asked, staring at the buttons of his shirt. He'd gotten dressed in a hurry and buttoned the wrong holes. His hair was sticking up in all directions, and he quickly tucked in his shirt. "It looks like you fell off a truck or out of bed." I swallowed hard as I stared at his attire.

"Yeah, sorry about that," he said nervously, glancing over his shoulder.

I ignored the hollow feeling in my stomach and called the server over and ordered another round of drinks.

"I can't stay," he said, while remaining standing.

"What?" I yelled. "You just got here, and it's our anniversary," I said in a slightly softer tone so that the other patrons would stop staring.

"I know and I'm sorry." He glanced over his shoulder again. I peered around him. Outside in the distance, a woman stood beside a tree with her arms crossed over her chest, staring our way.

I leaned back in the chair and folded my arms. That sinking feeling became a raging inferno. And I wanted to jump over the table and rip his heart out. I blinked rapidly because I would not cry.

"I'm sorry—"

"Don't say you're sorry. Just spit it out." I croaked, not liking how desperate I sounded.

"It just happened." He exhaled and bowed his head. When he glanced up at me, his eyes glistened in the light. "I never wanted to hurt you. I'll tell you anything you want to know."

"Who is she?"

"She's a friend of a client. I first met her at a client's

meeting, then we bumped into each other a couple of days ago and we went for coffee. It escalated pretty quickly after that."

The back of my throat ached as I tried to swallow. When I finally found my voice, I spoke. "So you chose today, our six-month anniversary, to tell me you're fucking another woman?" I yelled. Other patrons glanced nervously our way, then quickly at their food when I asked if they wanted something.

"Shh," he mumbled, embarrassed by my outburst. "I wanted to tell you on Wednesday already, but you were in such a good mood. And then yesterday came and went. Then today I realized I couldn't lie to you anymore. I thought nothing would happen between Mindy and me, but it did, and I really like her."

"You like her more than the person you've been sleeping with for six months. Is she so much better than what I've given you?" I said through gritted teeth.

"It's not like that, Claire. Don't compare yourself to her. You are very different. I know I'm the ass," he said, glancing around. "I've paid for your dinner already. Order whatever you want. And I'll send over the rest of your stuff from my apartment tomorrow," he said clinically, like he'd rehearsed his speech for days and no longer felt anything. That the last six months of us being together meant nothing to him. That I was disposable; kicked to the curb like garbage.

I couldn't answer him. Tears welled in my eyes, my heart cracked, and I'd lost my appetite.

"I'm sorry," Erik said, turning around and left without glancing at me.

I tried not to see where he was going, but I did. I watched him snake his arm around her waist like he used to around me, and I burst into tears.

And I thought my day would be great—it was one of the worst.

The server darted over, offering me napkins. He set the two whiskeys down and offered to take my order. He'd over-heard my break-up and tried to console me. I swatted his hand away and told him to bring me the bottle of his finest whiskey and a seafood pasta dish. Erik was paying after all.

Three hours later, I stumbled out of the restaurant before they called the police. I may have thrown my empty plate at the manager, pushed over a table, and smashed a chair into the wall. I decided it was best for all if I left before Blaire needed to bail me out of jail.

Not wanting to go home to my dark, very empty, and depressing apartment. I crossed the street and headed for the park. I loved visiting parks as a kid, but as an adult I was way too busy. Erik never liked the outdoors, and I tried to do what he wanted.

"Ugh," I grumbled when I thought of Erik again. I was doing so well. The whiskey amnesia had almost worked. *Almost.* Until I thought of the park and the trees and how I wanted to go hiking, but Erik hated it. Then my thoughts swarmed around in my head of us in his apartment, then in mine. Then memories of us going to the movies or a restaurant surfaced. Our social life consisted mainly of visiting friends and doing mundane human things.

As much as I hated him and enjoyed doing those things. I didn't think I'd ever want to do them again. I never wanted to watch a movie again, eat out, or visit friends. All I wanted to do was mope and wallow in my misery. Misery loved company.

I staggered through the dark alley toward the gate leading to the park, tripped over trash, and landed on my hands and knees. I burst out laughing at my silliness and that I hadn't been drunk like this in years.

Using the wall to steady myself, I meandered through the entrance and fell again, but this time on soft grass. My thoughts sobered. Tears pricked at my eyes. The silence of the park deafening.

Casting an eye around the enormous park, I didn't hear any night calls of animals or stridulation of insects; I was utterly alone. There was nothing but emptiness fueled by my loneliness. And I let go. I gave in to the sadness, and bawled until my throat was hoarse, my face swollen and most probably red, and my nose in desperate need of a blow. I hadn't ugly-cried in years, but tonight it was necessary.

I allowed myself the time to mourn the loss of a boyfriend I thought I'd loved. He was the first man I took a chance on after I told myself *never again*. I would use this time to get it out of my system. To get over Erik and to never think of him, or our time together, again. Not wanting to become a walking disaster, I knew I had to move on.

I wiped away the irritating tears with the back of my hand, stood tall, raised my head, pushed my shoulders back and traversed farther into the play area. The smell of damp ground and freshly cut grass wafted in the air. But the dark shadows beyond the border left me wondering whether I'd made a mistake coming here.

There were still no animal or insect sounds, and the winds whispered through the trees, creating ominous sounds that caused my arms to pebble.

When my thoughts sobered me completely, I realized I

was in the same park where they had attacked Blaire. This happened about four years ago and they had almost killed her; two different were-animals had left her for dead. I wondered whether it was safe for me to be here at this godly hour.

Swallowing my nervousness, I headed toward the exit. But the door was now closed. I was sure I'd just used that door when dread flooded my system. Now I stood with clarity. A chill ran down my spine. I felt another presence behind me; the weight of its stare unbearable.

A low, rumbling growl echoed around me. The hairs on my body stood on end. The thought of becoming a predator's dinner left a nasty taste in my mouth, and I spun around, coming face to face with a large-ass wolf. He snarled at me, baring his large canines. Its hungry gaze wanting to feast on me.

I didn't understand why, but the first thing that popped into my head was the coffee shop. "Jason? Is that you?"

The were-wolf stepped closer, growled, and showed me his teeth and blood-soaked muzzle. His black coat glistened in the moonlight, and I thought I saw a red shine.

Swallowing my screams, I realized he'd been hunting, and I was next on his list.

I raised my arms to show I was unarmed and stepped backward. The wolf snapped its jaw and closed the distance. I didn't want to know how it felt between its jaws; I spun around and dashed toward the entrance on the other side of the park.

I didn't get far.

A heavy weight crashed on top of me and I kissed the dirt. My head smacked the sandy surface with a loud thud, the wolf's claws digging into my back as its enormous jaws clamped down on my shoulder. I screamed blue murder, hoping someone would assist.

Nobody arrived.

It bit down harder, it's huge teeth cutting more of my muscle and tissue. The pain seared through my back, burned through my veins, and tingled down to my toes.

I lay frozen, too scared to move in case it decided to rip its jaw from my body and took a large piece of me with it.

It was too dark and too late for anyone to venture out this side of the area, and I realized I needed to save myself. But in order to do that, I had to get this thing off me first or become human kibble.

"No!" I shrieked. With all my strength I turned over. The wolf unclenched its jaw from my shoulder and jumped off. But when I was on my back, it pounced on me again. He lay on top of me, pressing his large thing between my legs, and snapped its muzzle in my face. To protect myself, I raised my forearm, and he bit down. Hard.

For a moment my pulse raged in my ears, my heart thundered in my chest, and I closed my eyes. Tonight was one of the worst evenings, and to top it off, I was going to die. If I didn't do something, I would become this were-wolf's meal, and nobody would care that I was gone. My corpse would remain unclaimed and unnamed, and I'd have a pauper's burial. I was sure Blaire and Ralph would miss me and perhaps claim my body, but I'd only been working for them for five months. I didn't think they cared.

The surrounding air moved as the wind changed direc-tion. Thoughts of strength flooded me and I knew I couldn't give up. This was an evening from Hell and I'd like a refund. One particular thought swirled around in my small brain; I couldn't give up. I couldn't let Erik, the asshole, ruin my life, and I couldn't allow this asshole-beast to get the best of me—or eat me.

The wolf pressed his thing harder against my core as he salivated over my arm. His sharp clawed paws stood on either side of my head, and I felt his hot, foul breath against my cheeks. With his large head close to mine, I saw his hungry gray-colored eyes with flecks of green.

When I moved my arm, he clamped down harder. Bursts of pain shot up my shoulder and I cried out again. Anger raged through my veins and another burst of adrenaline coursed through my system and on instinct I shoved two of my fingers into one of his eyes, gripped the squishy organ, and ripped it out.

The wolf yelped, letting go of my forearm, and moved away from me as it tried to assess its wound. I used the opportunity to ram my fist into its jaw. A loud snap sounded, and I kicked him in the balls. The wolf fell over, affording me the chance I desperately needed, and moved farther away from him. I cradled my injured arm against my chest and sprinted for the exit.

I glanced over my shoulder, but the big, bad wolf had disappeared. If it wasn't for the pain lacing my body, I would've thought I'd dreamed it all.

With adrenaline still coursing through my veins, I ran as fast as I could until I reached my apartment complex doors and entered the building.

Everything was a blur; running across the park toward my apartment block and entering my apartment. I couldn't recall how I got home. I was just grateful I arrived here without any other incident.

Once inside my apartment, I slammed the door shut, and dead bolted the locks. With my back against the door, I stood motionless. My body trembled until I could no longer stand, and I crashed to the floor in a heap of limp limbs and more tears.

I flinched when my shoulder touched the door, and I realized I should've gone to the emergency room. I couldn't leave now; the beast could be out there waiting for me. Not wanting to leave the safety of my apartment, I leaned on my good arm and stood with a grunt. My head swirled now that the adrenaline started tapering off. Every part of my body ached; my shoulder throbbed and burned while my forearm felt raw and exposed to the elements.

I glanced at myself in the bathroom mirror and recoiled. Mud caked my face and body where I'd fallen on my front and back. And the beast had torn chunks of flesh from my shoulder and forearm and had ripped my clothing. My bra was on its last thread, my makeup had smudged across my eyes and cheeks from crying, and my hair was knotty and messy. It amazed me nobody had seen me in this condition. But as I thought about it, I couldn't recall seeing anyone as I dashed through the streets.

Desperately wanting to clean myself of the wolf's saliva and scum, I undressed, wincing every step of the way. Slowly, I climbed into the shower. The scorching water splashed against my aching body. My shaking limbs eased as the warm water caressed every inch of me.

I allowed myself to cry in the quiet of my bathroom. This would be the last time, I promised myself. I wouldn't cry over Erik ever again. And I vowed to hunt down the beast who'd bitten me.

Grab your copy...
www.vinci-books.com/wolf

About the Author

A Multi-genre author writing twisted endings...

N Gray is a USA Today Bestselling Author who lives in Cape Town, South Africa, with her daughter and adopted cat named Miss Beans.

During the day, she's an analyst and provider profiler for a medical insurance company. At night, she types on her curved keyboard, creating fictional characters some may love and others you want to kill yourself.

She writes in four genres: urban fantasy, thriller, horror, and paranormal romance.

She now writes under Natalie Michaels for her new thrillers and SD Syns for her new horrors.

Acknowledgments

With special thanks to Rabea and Karin.

A special shout-out to *Tammy at Book Nook Nuts* for helping me find the gremlins.

And thank you to my readers, old and new, for taking a chance on my books. You are the reason I write the stories I do. As long as you keep reading, I'll keep writing. I'm truly humbled by your support and encouragement.

Thank you to my readers, old and new, for taking a chance on my books.

You are the reason I write the stories I do. As long as you keep reading, I'll keep writing.

I'm truly humbled by your support and encouragement.

I write in as many genres as I love reading in. There are so many stories swarming inside my head that I could never just choose one.

Horror is my guilty pleasure. I love writing short stories filled with dark humour and the occult, with a twist ending.

Urban fantasy and paranormal romance are where I love to spend my time, and I have so many books planned that I don't have enough time *(but I'll get there)*.

And lastly, my thrillers. Who doesn't love sitting on the edge of their seat while reading about what goes on inside the antagonist's mind? Well, I love writing about them.